C000150301

LOVE YOUR QUEEN

BOOK TWO

PENELOPE SKY

HARTWICK PUBLISHING

Hartwick Publishing
Love Your Queen
Copyright © 2017 by Penelope Sky
All Rights Reserved

I didn't want to admit this out loud because it made me weak, but Crewe was always adamant until he got what he wanted. "I'm a little nervous about flying…"

Instead of making fun of me, he tried to console me. "The pilot is excellent, as well as the rest of the crew. This jet is only a few years old. Everything is in perfect condition. Have a glass of wine and relax."

"Okay." I opened the shade and looked out the window, feeling my stomach do somersaults. We hadn't even taken off yet, and I felt woozy.

The plane lined up on the runway then took off. The powerful jets sent us high into the sky at a drastic angle. Higher and higher we climbed until we broke the cloud bank and reached an immense altitude.

Crewe read emails on his phone like nothing was happening. Ariel did the same.

I forced myself to remain calm and lean back against the seat. I hated showing weakness to anyone, even people I considered close friends. It was one of my stipulations.

We finally leveled out, and the plane cruised at a fixed speed. The constant hum of the air outside the plane filled the cabin, as well as the sound of the motors on either side of the plane.

If it stayed like this until we reached Italy, I could keep my cool. After everything I'd been through, it was a little ridiculous that I was afraid of flying. If we crashed right now, I wouldn't be a prisoner anymore.

That was the bright side of it.

With a sudden jolt, the plane dipped drastically. We dropped dozens of feet downward, my stomach suddenly feeling weightless.

"Oh god." I gripped the armrests and stifled the scream that naturally wanted to come out of my mouth. Adrenaline spiked in my blood, and I felt both sick and terrified at the exact same time.

Crewe looked at me, unaffected by the sudden jerk of the plane.

I tried to cover up my terror by looking out the window, not wanting him to know just how uncomfortable I was. He wouldn't give me any pity, especially for something he would deem stupid.

To my surprise, he grabbed my hand on the armrest and held it. "Turbulence is only caused by the mixing of hot and cold air. So when the plane shakes, that doesn't mean we're about to crash. It's normal, Lovely." He placed his phone in his pocket and directed his stare on me. "Alright?"

"I know..."

He grabbed my chin and tilted my face toward him. He just shaved that morning, so his face was smooth and hairless. It showed off his rugged mouth better than usual. "Eyes on me."

I did as he asked, mainly because I didn't know what else to do.

"I love Scotland. It's always been my home. But there are a few places in the world that feel like home too. Italy is one of them. I love the Tuscan heat, the ripe tomatoes, the wine even though I hardly drink any, and the ancient beauty of it all. You know the Colosseum is two thousand years old?"

Crewe was a man of few words, so sharing this story with me was out of character. "Are you trying to distract me?"

"Yeah," he answered. "Is it working?"

It was a kind gesture, especially from a man who possessed very little kindness. "Yeah."

"The first time I went to Rome was when I was eighteen. I took off with some of my friends to blow off some steam. We partied a lot, met beautiful women, and drank more wine than our stomachs could handle. Ever since then, I've always loved to visit. But I admit my visits are a lot more low-key now."

I wondered what he looked like when he was eighteen. That was almost half the age he was now. "Sounds like fun. Finley must have been worried."

"I drove him crazy when I was growing up. He definitely prefers me as an adult."

The plane kept shaking, and Ariel sipped her wine like she didn't even notice.

Crewe carried on the conversation. "We're staying at one of my villas in Tuscany. It's quiet and remote. You'll like it."

"It'll be a big change from Scotland."

"It'll take some time to get used to the heat." He kept his fingers around me, his courage seeping into my veins from the contact of our skin. Seeing him so relaxed made me feel better, made me think we weren't in any imminent danger. There was no way a powerful man like

Crewe would allow a plane crash to claim his life. "You can enjoy the sunshine and the pool while I take care of business."

"How long will we be there?"

"A week at the most. Business with the Barsetti brothers is pretty easy. I usually stick around for a few extra days because it's a long flight."

The plane began to shake less and less. Eventually, it felt smooth. The jet glided through the sky, the sound of the air outside the plane the only indicator we were tens of thousands of feet in the air.

My hand loosened around his, and my body finally relaxed. Despite my background in science, the concept of flying across the world had always troubled me. I was always afraid something in the engine would go wrong, or the pilot would make an honest mistake that would send us all to our deaths. I rested my head against the leather cushion and let out a deep breath.

Crewe watched me. "Feeling better?"

"I'm just glad the plane stopped shaking."

He pulled his hand away, making me feel lonely without his touch. I didn't need him to hold my hand to make me feel better, but the second it was gone, I missed it. It was nice to have someone comfort me. "Nothing to be scared of. Planes fly all over the world, and there are rarely any crashes. And my planes definitely won't crash."

"Stop saying the word *crash*."

He smiled. "Sorry, that was a bit insensitive."

"It's okay… I know you're trying to help."

He pulled his phone out of his pocket again and checked his email.

I shut the window shade because I didn't want to see the endless blue. It would only remind me how high up we were. "How long is the flight?"

"Pretty long. Try to get some sleep."

I automatically leaned against his shoulder to get comfortable even though I could easily recline back. Something about the fabric of his shirt and the warmth of his skin made me feel better. Now I was used to sleeping with him every night. He was the silent lullaby that sent me to my dreams.

He positioned me upward then put the armrests away, so there was nothing separating us. "Lie in my lap. It'll be more comfortable that way."

This was the nicest he'd ever been to me. He defended me against Dunbar and Ariel, but he never went out of his way to put my comfort before his own. "Are you sure?"

"Yeah. You know how much I like having my lap near your mouth anyway." He wore that cocky grin I'd become accustomed to.

I rolled my eyes then lowered myself onto his lap. I caught Ariel staring at us from her seat across the row, probably wondering why Crewe was letting me lie across his lap. I ignored her and got comfortable.

When I was across his lap, Crewe rested his arm over my waist. "Need a blanket?"

"I'm okay." I pulled my knees to my chest because I was a little cold.

Crewe must have caught my lie because he turned to Ariel. "Grab me a blanket, please."

"You're kidding, right?" she countered.

I couldn't see Crewe's expression, but I imagined he was giving her an intimidating look. "You wanna keep your job, right?"

Crewe was just going to make Ariel hate me more. I wasn't sure why she disliked me so much. It wasn't a big deal that I was lying across his lap. He fucked me every night, so this was pretty tame.

Ariel stood up and opened the overhead compartment. She tossed a blanket at us, the fabric landing right on top of my head. "There you are, *Your Highness*."

I felt the tension rise like heat from a fire.

Crewe didn't say anything, but I knew his silence was threatening enough. He wouldn't let anyone get away with that kind of back talk. There would be repercussions later. He probably just didn't want to go to war with her in a concealed vessel with his men in the back of the plane.

Crewe returned his attention to his phone like nothing just happened. His jaw was clenched in irritation, but he swallowed his anger. His arm rested around my waist, his touch warm and preferable to the ice-cold air coming out of the vents.

I thought I wouldn't be able to sleep when I was so nervous, but within minutes, my eyes grew heavy and closed. I drifted off to sleep with Crewe's lap acting as a pillow, feeling unusually comfortable despite all the calamity surrounding the ride.

2

CREWE

The plane touched down, and I was escorted into the back of an SUV at the airport. London was drowsy from sleeping on the plane, and she continued to lean on me for support. She'd never been affectionate or clingy before, so I let the closeness slide. When she was scared on the plane, I felt obligated to calm her down. After everything I put her through, it was the least I could do.

But Ariel wasn't having it.

It was nighttime when we arrived in Italy, so there wasn't much to see during the car ride. London hooked her arm through mine and rested her head against my shoulder while I continued to handle emails and text messages.

Ariel sat against the other window, wearing a permanent sneer on her pretty face.

We arrived at my villa an hour later and passed through the gates. I had an acre of land with nothing but grass and oak trees, but the privacy was nice. It wasn't as remote as my home in the Shetland Islands, but it was beautiful nonetheless. The two-story house was big enough for me and my team, giving me the luxury of having most of the top floor to myself. I didn't have to keep quiet when my ladies came to visit.

London finally woke up when we arrived. She stood in front of the house and examined it despite the darkness. There weren't streetlights in Tuscany since it was rural countryside. Features were difficult to make out, and the guys had to break out their flashlights to find the entryway. "I can't see much…but it looks nice."

"Wait until the sun comes up." We walked inside, and my team carried the luggage exactly where it needed to go. Ariel stepped off to the side and made a phone call, probably returning all the calls she missed during the flight.

I hadn't slept on the plane, so I was tired. I was ready to have a few glasses of scotch in front of the fireplace in my bedroom to wind down. Then I'd fuck London before I went to bed. Business could resume when the sun came up.

But I had to take care of something first.

London lingered in my proximity, not exploring the rest of the house without my permission. She was getting better with obedience, learning to follow my commands without my actually giving them. Like a new puppy, she was slowly being trained.

"Lovely."

She faced me, her hair messy from sleeping in my lap during the flight. She was a low-maintenance woman who required little upkeep to remain beautiful. It was the only time I'd witnessed such a thing. Josephine spent more time perfecting her appearance than anyone I knew. Since she was royalty, I understood the necessity. But after looking at London every day, I realized appearances meant nothing. She was far more beautiful than most women I knew, without lifting a finger. Not too many women could say that.

But I would never tell her that. "Wait for me upstairs. Third door on the left."

"Why?"

My eyes narrowed.

She immediately understood this was one of those times when I wanted to be obeyed without question. She didn't ask any more questions and took the stairs to the second landing. The rest of the men finished unloading the car then took their positions around the perimeter.

Ariel hung up her call.

No one was around, and we finally had the privacy I'd been waiting for. "Ariel, as much as I need you to stick around, I'm not gonna put up with that bullshit again. When I ask you to do something, you do it. Or you can find someone else to sign your checks. You understand me?"

She crossed her arms over her chest, wearing the same irritated look on her face as earlier. She had an astute business mind, and she understood all the tiny cogs in the machinery I'd built. There was no one better to have as a business partner. She had a brilliant brain and a fierce attitude. But I refused to be disrespected like that.

"We've always had a great business relationship. Suddenly, London comes around, and everything I value about our partnership goes out the window. I don't know what your problem is, so you need to tell me." I wondered if she was jealous seeing me with another woman. In all the years we'd been working together, I'd never suspected she saw me as anything more than a business partner and friend. There was never any attraction between us, any sort of chemistry. I'd never made a pass at her because I didn't mix business with pleasure. She seemed to share my same ideology. But if that wasn't it, I couldn't figure it out.

"I've seen you with your women. You're cold, heartless, and right to the point."

I stared at her blankly, unsure why she was stating the obvious.

"But when this woman comes around, everything changes. You didn't hand her over to Bones like you planned, and she's sleeping in your bed every night. It's none of my business who you fuck, and I really don't care about your sex life, but this woman can't turn into something more. And it seems like it's going in that direction. We both know there's a very small pool of women you can spend the rest of your life with. London isn't on the list."

Now everything made sense. "That's what you've been worried about?" I had to hold back my laughter because it was ridiculous. "If that's what the problem is, we don't have a problem. London is something I keep around for entertainment. That's it."

"But you can't keep her around forever."

"I realize that." I had no idea what I was going to do with her eventually. "And I don't intend to. She's just like all the others. Don't worry about that."

Ariel didn't seem entirely convinced. "You're different with her. I've seen it."

"No, I'm not. I comforted her on the plane because she was scared. Doesn't mean I love the woman."

"But it doesn't mean you're indifferent either. Have you been with other women since she's come along?"

I refused to answer that question. "You're approaching a line you shouldn't cross."

"I'm not being nosy. I'm just proving my point."

Ariel knew a lot about me. She probably figured out I hadn't been chasing tail lately. "It doesn't matter. London doesn't mean anything to me. I'm not going to repeat myself."

She searched my gaze as if she was searching for a lie. Ariel was invested in my personal life because my future marriage affected her. If I'd married Josephine like I originally planned, it would have been easy to expand my scotch business into foreign territories. Ariel would be much richer in that scenario than she was now. Not to mention, it opened a lot of other doors for her as well. If I ended up with a nobody, then she had very little room to advance professionally. We were both ambitious businesspeople, determined to grow our wealth as much as possible. "You give me your word, Crewe?"

She knew my word meant more than anything else in the world. "Yes, I give you my word."

London had already showered by the time I arrived in the bedroom. She opened the Mediterranean doors to the balcony and stood at the railing. She looked into the darkness surrounding the house, only seeing the stars because everything else was invisible. She stood in one of my t-shirts with just her panties underneath.

"Wait until you see it in the morning." I undressed and tossed my clothes on the hardwood floor. I'd been wearing the same thing for hours, and I was eager to shower and appreciate a bottle of scotch.

She came back inside and shut the doors behind her. "I can tell it's beautiful without seeing anything. The air is nice…reminds me of home."

I was sure she was homesick all the time, but I never felt bad for her. She didn't have freedom, but she still had the opportunity to see the world on my dime. I scooped some ice cubes into a glass and poured some scotch.

London eyed my action judgmentally. "Crewe, you've been drinking all day."

"I'm aware."

"Just some friendly advice, step it down a notch."

"Noted." I downed half the glass before I returned it to the counter. "I'm gonna get in the shower. When I get out, I expect to see you naked on the bed with your ass in the air. Got it?" I didn't want to talk for the rest of the night. I just wanted to fuck her from behind and stare at that beautiful little asshole then go to sleep.

A fire always leapt in her eyes when I told her what to do, but she invariably controlled her mouth. "Yes, sir."

I knew it was so hard for her to answer that way, and knowing she struggled made me hard. I loved conquering an unconquerable woman. It gave me the kind of power I craved, the kind of undeniable control I needed constantly. I turned to walk into the shower.

"Can I ask something?"

I turned around even though I shouldn't have. I stared her down and silently gave her permission to speak her mind.

"Is everything okay with Ariel?"

Ariel was focused on business and business alone. That was why I liked her so much, trusted her instincts as completely as my own. "We worked it out."

She slowly nodded, obviously wanting more detail than that. "What's her problem with me? Maybe there's something I can do to annoy her less."

There was nothing London could do to annoy her less. London would have to stop being beautiful, stop stealing my focus, and stop being the ornery spitfire that she was. All the women I encountered were poised and refined, always behaving with class that was borderline boring.

London would have to change everything about herself. "No."

I woke up the next morning with London on her side of the bed. We fucked every night before we slept, but we never cuddled. She always stuck to her side of the bed, and I stuck to mine.

Which was how I preferred it.

I showered then got dressed just when she woke up.

She sat up and stretched her arms over her head, the sheets falling and revealing her perfect rack. Her hair was a mess from the way she rolled around, and the sleep was heavy in her eyes. Her gaze immediately went to the window, which was covered by the curtain.

I read her thoughts and pulled on the string so she could see the view. The Tuscan hillside immediately became apparent, the green grass and the distant vineyards easy to see.

She stared with wide eyes, taking in her first sight of the beautiful country.

I opened the door and found my breakfast tray on the ground where I instructed my chef to leave it. Two coffees and two breakfast plates were prepared for me and my guest. I carried it to the table and sat down.

London's eyes followed me. "Can I join you?"

I nodded and sipped my coffee.

She pulled on one of my shirts that was left on the ground then sat across from me. Her brown hair was wavy but still soft. Her green eyes were a lot more vibrant now that she had a full night of sleep. She cupped her mug with both hands before she inhaled the steam.

I watched every move. "What are you doing?"

"What?"

"Are you smelling the coffee?"

She took a drink before she set it down. "So? I like the smell of coffee."

She looked so cute when she did it, but I refused to tell her that.

"People smell wine before they drink it."

True. I wasn't a big wine drinker, so I'd never personally done it.

"What's on the agenda today?"

I cut into my egg whites. "I'm meeting with my suppliers this afternoon. Need a few things."

"Am I joining you?"

I never mixed business with pleasure. "No."

"So what am I going to do? Stay here all afternoon?"

"Yep."

Her face contorted into one of annoyance. "I'm in a beautiful place. I'd like to see more of it."

"Meeting my suppliers isn't going to facilitate that."

"It's better than being stuck in here. You know I'm not going to wander when Dunbar is hanging around."

I drank my coffee. "I know he's a bit ominous, but he would never seriously hurt you—unless you deserved it."

"His standards for punishment are much lower than yours." She drank her coffee then stared bleakly at her breakfast. "Seriously, this looks like shit."

"It's good for you."

"There's no fat."

"Fat isn't good for you."

"Actually, that's incorrect. We need good fat to help us burn bad fat. We all need protein, carbs, and fat. Without one, you'd be missing a corner of the pyramid, and it would come toppling down."

Sometimes I forgot she was training to be a doctor before I stole her. "What kind of doctor were you training to be?"

"I was in medical school before you took me, not residency. So I hadn't made a decision yet."

I didn't have any idea what she was talking about, but I didn't let her know that. "And what would you like your decision to be?"

She pushed her eggs around without taking a bite. "Emergency room medicine."

"Why?" My universe focused on diplomacy, royalty, and business. I never took an interest in any other discipline, whether it was law or medicine. I lived in my own little world, and I liked it that way.

She shrugged. "Personal reasons." She pushed the food around again. "Man, I miss Finley."

I ignored the last thing she said. "What personal reasons?"

She kept her eyes down. "I don't want to talk about it."

"Then why did you bring it up?"

"I didn't." She looked up, her mood souring. "You're the one asking all these questions."

"And you've been answering them until now."

"I just don't want to, okay? It's not like you tell me everything."

"You're my slave. I don't have to tell you anything."

"I'm not a slave," she hissed. "Don't call me that."

"I can call you whatever I want. Now answer me."

It looked like her eyes were about to explode with rage. "Why do you care? You've never taken an interest in my personal life. Why are you so curious?"

Good question. "Just answer the damn question."

She knew she couldn't push me any further. If she did, her brother's life would be on the line. Coercion was the best way to keep her in line, even if I was just bluffing. "My parents were killed by a drunk driver when I was eight. They were pinned to a tree and died on impact. It wouldn't have mattered if the ambulance had gotten there sooner or if a better doctor were on staff that night. But maybe I could make a difference to someone someday."

My fingers were still wrapped around the handle to my mug, but I didn't take a drink. My food remained untouched, and I stopped breathing. Inexplicable pain washed over me when I heard her confession. I pictured her as an eight-year-old getting the news that her parents had been killed by someone who drank too much. Joseph was just a few years older than her, so he didn't understand what was going on either. Unsuspecting pain throbbed in my chest, and I actually pitied the woman sitting across from me.

I lost my parents. So did she.

I didn't know what to say. I had the urge to hug her, to say something to console her for her loss. But I sat rigid and still, unable to think of an appropriate action. I didn't want her to assume I cared, so I did everything I could to make it seem like I didn't give a damn at all.

She looked away when nothing was forthcoming.

She showed me sympathy when I told her about my parents. It wouldn't be inappropriate if I expressed the same understanding. It didn't mean I cared about her as a person. It just meant I wasn't a complete asshole. "I'm sorry, Lovely."

When she looked up, she couldn't hide her surprise. Maybe she expected me to be rude like I usually was.

"Looks like we have more in common than I realized."

"Yeah...seems like it." She ran her hand through her hair, pulling it from her face and fluffing it up in the back. She finally took a bite of her food and didn't hide the cringe that emerged across her face. "Seriously, how do you eat this crap?"

"I have a waistline to maintain. Don't act like you don't enjoy it."

She rolled her eyes and took another bite. She was probably hungry from not eating much the day before and fasting the entire night. She could either eat now or not eat until I returned from my meeting. "You aren't that hot."

I raised an eyebrow. "Oh, yeah?"

"Yeah."

I didn't buy that at all. "Sure seems like you think I'm hot."

"You aren't bad to look at it. But hot? No."

I could see the lie in her eyes. "Whatever you say, Lovely. I make you come every time we fuck, so I must be doing something right."

She took another bite and dodged the statement altogether.

"I think you're gorgeous." I wasn't ashamed to say that. When we first met, I didn't care for her. But the longer she talked back to me, the more attitude she showed, the more my attraction grew. I loved that fire in her eyes. I loved that sassiness she showed when anyone crossed her. I adored her fearlessness.

Her guard slowly dropped once my confession had been made. Daggers weren't in her eyes, and she actually seemed to like me—for an instant. "Okay...I do think you're hot."

I grinned from ear-to-ear at my victory. "You didn't need to tell me that because I already knew. But thanks anyway." I grabbed the newspaper that was sitting on the tray and opened it.

"I want to ask you something."

"Yes?"

"Everywhere you go, you have a million people with you."

"More like a dozen, but what's your point?"

"Are you ever alone? Like, truly alone?"

I couldn't remember the last time I went anywhere without a guard flanking me. Once my parents were killed, I was under special custody of Finley and other guards. I grew into a man with an army surrounding me at all times. The only privacy I had was when I met women for dates and good sex. "I guess not."

"Does that bother you?"

Yes. No. I went back and forth. "It's a small price to pay for protection."

"I don't think I could live like that…"

"You're a solitary person?"

"No. But I value my independence. Sometimes I need to be alone to clear my mind. If I had people around me all the time, I'd go crazy."

"You've been doing pretty well for the past three months." When she wasn't under my supervision, my guards were watching her. She didn't have much alone time even in my bedroom.

Her eyes gleamed with irritation. "It's a daily struggle…"

I glanced at the clock on the wall and knew I needed to get going. I took another bite of my breakfast and set my paper aside even though I didn't get the chance to read it. "I'll see you when I get back."

"No, I'm coming with you." She stood up, like that would make a difference.

"No." I grabbed my jacket off the hanger in the closet and threw it on, completing my three-piece suit.

"I don't want to stay here with your men. I told you they make me uncomfortable."

"Too bad."

She walked up to me with her hands on her hips, making up for her lack of height with her attitude. "Are you planning on keeping me forever?"

I didn't have a clue what I was going to do with her. The impulse to keep her instead of handing her over to Bones was inexplicable. I didn't know exactly what changed my mind. Now that I'd changed my plans, I didn't know how to proceed with her. I could fuck her all I wanted, but eventually, I would grow tired of her and move on with my life. But I couldn't just let her go. I couldn't let the world know I turned soft. "Maybe."

"Then you can't treat me like a dog. Put me to good use. You know I'm smart. I can hold my own even when I'm outnumbered. I've got an ass that won't quit. You can get more use out of me by including me than leaving me here alone."

"I think most women would love to stay behind and drink wine and eat chocolate all day." If she played her cards right, she could be well taken care of for the rest of her life. All she had to do was not piss me off.

"I don't want to sit on my ass all day and get fat. I need more than that."

"You aren't of any use to me."

"I like scotch. Maybe I can help you with your business."

"This meeting has nothing to do with my distillery." It was about the underworld. It was about revenge for all the people who had the audacity to fuck with me.

"Crewe, come on."

I didn't know what her angle was. "You think if you learn about all my criminal activities, you'll be able to turn me in one day? I could tell you every little thing about me, let you go, and the police still wouldn't do a damn thing about it."

"What makes you so sure?"

"Because I own the police." I owned most of the world. Now I just needed to own my enemies.

Her eyes shifted back and forth as she looked at me. "Turning you in isn't on my itinerary anyway."

"Really?" I asked sarcastically. "After everything I've done to you?"

"I'm not saying kidnapping me is okay. But I think you've got a soul underneath this façade. If you didn't have a heart, you would have handed me over to Bones."

I couldn't let her think I ever gave a damn about her. I couldn't let her believe I showed an ounce of compassion. If I did, all the rules would go out the window. She would try to backstab me in the middle of the night because she knew I would never retaliate. She could push me in directions I never wanted to go. "I didn't give you away because I wanted to make Joseph suffer even more. I wanted him to know his little sister is being fucked every night—by his greatest enemy. My heart died a long time ago, Lovely. All you see now is flesh and bones."

"Your car is ready, sir," Dunbar said in the entryway.

I adjusted my cuff links. "Thank you."

"How many men would you like to accompany you?"

I adjusted my sleeves then buttoned the front of my suit. "None." London's words didn't get to me. The Barsetti brothers were harmless when unprovoked. They probably wouldn't even be armed.

Dunbar raised an eyebrow but didn't question me, knowing that was suicide. "You know where to reach me."

I nodded then walked to the door.

"Hold up." London's voice sounded from behind me. "I'm coming too."

I wanted to snap her neck. I turned around and gave her a merciless glare, annoyed she defied me right in front of my men.

She read my look without an ounce of fear. "I'm not staying cooped up like a chicken."

"You think these guys are gonna save you or something?" I didn't understand why she wanted to accompany me so much. When we were in Scotland, she didn't try to follow me around everywhere. She stayed in her bedroom in the castle until I finished my day and returned to her.

"No." She stepped closer to me and lowered her voice so only I could hear her. "I don't want to be stuck with Dunbar and Ariel…who both hate me with every fiber of their beings. The only person I feel remotely safe around is you."

The hair on the back of my neck prickled in a way it never had before. Her confession soothed my ego, stoked my confidence. I should be annoyed that she thought of me as protection rather than danger, but I wasn't. Perhaps it was the fact that she was wearing skin-tight jeans and a black top that made her tits look incredible, but something about her was getting to me. "You shouldn't feel safe with me."

"At least I know what I'm getting with you. There're no surprises. No sudden turns. If I follow the rules, everything will stay the same. You won't hurt me or Joseph. Dunbar is unpredictable. He wants to hurt me just for the sake of it. And Ariel...if I were in trouble, she wouldn't do anything to stop it. She would just look the other way."

Her characterization of my two employees was dead-on, but they were far too loyal to betray me. If London annoyed them, they might push her to the side or ignore her. But they would never take it further than that.

London stood on her tiptoes then pressed her lips to mine. It might have been her last plan to persuade me, to kiss me and soften my calloused heart. Her sweet lips moved with mine, and she gave me some of her tongue, giving me a playful lick that made the rest of my skin tingle. Her arm moved around my neck, and she kissed me in front of my men, making me hard in my slacks.

My arm circled her petite waist, and her sinister plan worked. I didn't hold my ground because I no longer cared. When those perky tits were pressed against me and her tongue tangled with mine, I became a different man. Her kiss was different from the kind I shared with most women. Perhaps she was just a good kisser, or maybe it was because she was so unattainable. Whenever I fought her, she fought harder. She had a smartass comment to make in retaliation to everything I said. But I finally earned her cooperation. That made her more valuable than all my other women combined.

Because I was a sick bastard.

She finished the kiss then breathed gently into my mouth, the smell of her hair complimenting her naturally addictive fragrance.

Now that I was hard, I didn't want her to leave my side. My men saw that little performance, and I didn't want to leave my toy behind and give them the wrong idea. I wanted to pull over on the drive, have her suck my dick, and then continue on with my life. "Let's go."

Victory shone in her eyes now that she was getting her way.

"But don't try anything." I didn't need to finish the threat.

"I won't."

———

We arrived at the Barsetti estate, a three-story mansion with vineyards on either side of it. The black gates opened as I approached, and I circled the fountain in the center and the valet parked my car.

London stood beside me and looked up at the magnificent house with green ivy growing over the walls. The Mediterranean style windows were open, letting fresh air enter the multiple bedrooms upstairs.

When I reached the door, it opened before I could knock.

"Good afternoon, Mr. Donoghue. I'm Lars." An older man in a gray suit gave me a quick bow. He looked like the butler of the house, reminding me of Finley but with fancier clothes. "Mr. Barsetti and Mr. Barsetti are expecting you in the drawing room." He turned to London, clearly not expecting her to accompany me.

"I'm sorry, Lars. This is Lady London. I should have mentioned I was bringing her today." Even though there would have only been a thirty-minute warning.

"Lady London, it's a pleasure to have you." Lars ushered us inside. "I know the men prefer scotch. Can I get you the same, or would you rather have something else?"

"Scotch is fine," she said with a smile. "Thank you, Lars."

I stared at her in surprise.

"Let me show you the way." Lars walked in front and led us to the drawing room on the second floor.

I eyed London, watching her every move.

She turned to me when she noticed my stare. "What?"

"You're beautiful like a flower, but you drink like a man."

"Your point?"

I grabbed her hand. "No point at all." I may have to pour a bottle of scotch all over her body and lick it away when we get home. I'd lick it out of every opening on her body. Her nipples would taste even better coated in the amber liquid.

We entered the drawing room, and I walked inside first when I would normally show my manners by letting London step inside before me. The two brothers sat on different couches in front of the fire. A bottle of iced scotch sat on the table along with three glasses. The men were already drinking. I would have been disappointed if they weren't.

"I'll return with hors d'oeuvres." Lars bowed before he returned to the door.

"We don't need any food, Lars," Crow said. "Men just want to drink."

London cleared her throat. "I'm not gonna turn down some homemade Italian cooking."

Lars smiled like that made him happier than he'd been in a long time. "On the way." He walked out.

Crow and Cane both stared at her, obviously not noticing her until then.

"My apologies," Crow said. "Didn't realize a lady was joining us. What can I get you, sweetheart?"

I didn't hide my glare, offended he called my woman by such an endearment. "She'll have scotch—like the rest of us." I took a seat and tapped the cushion next to me, telling her exactly where I wanted her.

The second her ass was on the cushion, my hand moved to her thigh, and I crossed her legs. I shouldn't care if

Crow and Cane found her attractive. She didn't mean anything to me anyway.

But I did care.

Crow smiled before he opened the bottle. "My apologies." He poured two glasses and handed them over.

I handed London hers even though she could have reached it herself. It was an unnecessary act of possession, but Crow and Cane weren't typical criminals. They were both handsome and wealthy. "This is London. London, this is Crow." I held up my glass and aimed it in his direction. "And that's Cane."

Crow nodded in acknowledgment. He was the older brother with the winery, while Cane was in charge of their arms business. They laundered their money through their clean business, just the way I did with my scotch.

"Pleasure to make your acquaintance." Cane's eyes settled on her a little longer than I preferred.

I shouldn't have brought her.

"Where's Ariel?" Crow asked.

"Working." I didn't have to explain where my business partner was. I handled all the deals while she worked in the dark. That was how the arrangement went. Sometimes I brought her along. Sometimes I didn't.

"I was hoping London was her replacement," Cane said.

Cane wasn't a fan of Ariel. Probably because she didn't put up with his sleazy lines and sexist comments. "London is my personal property." I wouldn't call her my woman because that would imply she meant a great deal to me. But I wouldn't use the word slave because London would have an outburst.

"Oh…even better." Cane winked.

Crow glared at his brother before he turned to me. "Let's talk business. That's what we're here for, right?"

I always preferred Crow. He got right to the point and didn't ask too many questions. "Let's."

Cane left the room to take a call, and London walked to the large windows on the other side of the room to admire the view of the vineyards and the pool. It was just Crow and me for a brief time.

"How's business?" I knew he would give me a rehearsed answer since we never revealed our secrets to one another.

"No complaints. You?"

I smiled. "No complaints." I knew he had a blood feud with one of my clients, so I never mentioned his name while we were together. I considered myself to be a neutral businessman who didn't have any emotional investment in my clients. They bought what I was selling, or they didn't. End of story.

Crow nodded to London on the other side of the room. "Josephine is long gone, huh?"

I didn't like to speak of that woman, but all of Western Europe knew of my engagement. I'd never been so humiliated in my life. She left me for a man with a better chance at the throne, spitting on my legacy and everything I had to offer. It probably wouldn't have hurt so much if I'd never loved the bitch.

But I did.

The Russians destroyed my family, and that British cunt destroyed my name. Now I needed revenge on two fronts, and I would get it one way or another. I wouldn't let anyone step on me ever again. I wouldn't let anyone get close to my heart again. Whoever I married would only be a match of convenience, someone who could give me children to carry on my legacy.

But that was it.

"Yeah." I masked my discomfort by taking a drink of my scotch. I'd been working with Crow for years, but I wouldn't consider us to be friends. Good acquaintances, perhaps. People like us didn't really have friends. "She came by a few weeks ago and said she made a mistake. Wanted another chance."

"That's some nerve…"

I wouldn't take her back. I was over Josephine the moment she turned her back on me. Every feeling I had disappeared instantly. My heart became calloused and black, and I lost the ability to feel any form of happiness.

Now I just wanted blood.

"I'm glad she's miserable." It was a cold thing to say, but I really didn't care.

"That makes two of us." He clanked his glass against mine. "Your new plaything seems nice. I heard one of your clients crossed you…"

Good news traveled fast. "Yeah. I took his sister as payment."

Crow grinned. "You've gotta teach them a lesson. But I have to say…" He looked over his shoulder and glanced at her. "She doesn't seem like much of a prisoner."

"Meaning?" Because she was beautiful? Because she was one of the sexiest women I'd ever been with?

"If I were a prisoner, I wouldn't smile. I wouldn't drink scotch with a room full of men and enjoy it. She doesn't seem like she's being held against her will. It's almost as if she likes you." He crossed his legs and leaned back against the couch.

I watched her figure in the corner, treasuring the sight of her beautiful curves. She had an hourglass figure, something I'd always been a sucker for. I turned back to Crow. "I threatened to kill her brother if she doesn't obey me. I have a transmitter in his skull. The second she displeases me, I'll hit the button and give him a stroke."

Crow nodded like he was impressed. "You've got this all figured out."

"Let this be a lesson to you. Don't fuck with me."

He chuckled. "Wasn't planning on it." He glanced at London again. "Is she up for grabs?"

It wasn't uncommon for business partners to share women. I'd done it before myself. Since I made it clear she meant nothing to me, his question wasn't out of line. But I didn't want to loan her out. She was my pet, my prisoner. I didn't want to share her with any other man. "No."

Crow accepted my decision without argument. "Don't be offended if Cane asks you the same question."

"I won't. I'm surprised he hasn't asked already."

He chuckled. "You know my brother as well as I do. So why did you bring her, then?"

"She wanted to come along."

"Looking for an escape route, possibly?"

The more I thought about it, the more unlikely that seemed. "No. She knows I'm not bluffing about her brother."

"Maybe she just wanted to get out of the house, then."

"She doesn't like my men. Says she doesn't trust them."

"And she trusts you?" he asked with interest.

I shrugged, unsure how she felt. She wanted me to protect her from my staff, and that made me feel hard in a way I couldn't explain. Then she stuck her tongue in my mouth and chased all my logical thoughts away.

She had a magic touch.

"I think she trusts me in some aspects."

"Well, being by your side really is the safest place she could be, relatively speaking. She'll never be hungry, poor, or in any danger. But you aren't going to keep her forever, right?"

"Not sure yet."

"Well, are you gonna kill her when you're finished?"

That's what I should do. She would become useless to me eventually. I would meet another woman, or perhaps the woman I should marry, and then London would just be a burden. Obviously, I couldn't just let her go because she knew too much.

He was right. I would have to kill her. "I guess so."

3

LONDON

We drove back to his estate thirty minutes away. Crewe drove with one hand on the wheel, his eyes on the road straight ahead. His other hand rested in his lap, and dusk was slowly settling across Tuscany.

It was beautiful here. I loved the warm sun, the green vines of the vineyards, and the dusty dirt that flew into the air when we drove down the road. In some ways, it reminded me of home. In others, it didn't remind me of anything I'd seen in my lifetime.

Crewe didn't make small talk. He seemed to be in a bad mood, but I wasn't sure why. I behaved myself the entire time and rarely spoke unless I was spoken to first. I could have given a lot of smartass comments, but I didn't. I was just grateful to be with him instead of back at the house with his psychopath partner and his violent henchman.

I wasn't trying to run.

If I did, he would kill Joey. I didn't have any other option but to make the best of my situation. I wasn't sure how long I would be there. Maybe I would be there forever. If I could make him fall in love with me, he may leave Joey alone and let me go.

But the more I got to know him, the more unlikely that seemed.

Crewe was heartless.

He lost his family, and I knew something serious happened with Josephine. He carried too many scars, too much hatred. But at the same time, he did have his soft moments. He told me I was beautiful and told Dunbar to keep his hands off me. If he really didn't care, he wouldn't intervene.

And I still suspected he changed his mind about Bones for a different reason.

But I would never really know the truth about that.

"Why do I get the feeling you're mad?"

He kept his eyes on the road. "Because I am."

I should have been more specific. "Why do I get the feeling you're mad at *me*?"

"I'm not mad at you. I'm mad at myself for allowing you to come with me."

"Why?" I blurted. "I didn't do anything wrong."

"Crow asked if he could have a go with you." Crewe gripped the steering wheel tighter, his knuckles turning white. "Cane did the same."

I was grateful he didn't share me. Crow and Cane were good-looking, but I didn't want to be loaned out to strangers. It had been difficult enough for me to sleep with Crewe to begin with. Now sleeping with him was so natural I didn't think twice about it. "You didn't act like I meant anything special to you…"

Crewe clenched his jaw.

"And I don't mean anything to you, so why do you care?"

"I just do. I shouldn't have let you come. It was a stupid decision."

"You're being really unfair. I didn't do anything wrong. It's not my fault they're both perverts."

"They aren't perverts," he said quietly. "They're men. When men see a beautiful woman, they want to fuck her. It's pretty fucking natural." His jaw was still clenched as he spoke.

"Then you shouldn't be upset."

He turned his head my way, the anger radiating in his eyes.

That wasn't the smartest thing to say. "Crewe, if you're gonna keep me around for a long time, put me to use. Let me help with your business. Give me something to do. I don't want to be at the mercy of your employees every time you aren't around."

"I don't care how you feel, London. I'm sorry if that wasn't apparent."

I crossed my arms over my chest and looked out the window. "Why don't you just kill me?" I had hope prior to this, hope that something good would happen. But now, all optimism was disappearing.

He turned his head to look at me again.

"Just kill me," I repeated. "You'll get your vengeance on Joey. He'll be miserable. Win-win."

"Why would I do that when I enjoy being between your legs so much?"

My heartbeat quickened at his words, although I wasn't sure why. Did that simple sentence make me aroused? Was it the possessiveness? Or was it nothing at all, just a natural reaction.

I purposely kept my eyes out the window, not wanting to look at him or see his reaction to me. I didn't respond to his flirty words, refusing to do so.

His hand grabbed my elbow, and he loosened my arm before he grabbed my hand. He rested it on my thigh then brushed his thumb along my knuckles. Like he did on the plane, he showed me affection that surprised me. It was tender and sweet, a great contradiction to everything he was.

My heart rate slowed down again, and just for a moment, I felt at peace. I felt safe, like nothing could hurt me while he consoled me. I liked this version of Crewe, when he showed compassion that derived from nowhere.

"I'm not gonna kill you, Lovely. That's the last thing I want to do."

"Then what do you want to do with me?" I didn't pull my hand away because it felt nice. I wanted him to keep touching me. It made me feel alive, not hopeless and dead.

"For now, this." He brought my hand to his lips and kissed it. "That's all."

It wasn't an answer, but at least it wasn't a death threat. As long as I was useful to him, he would keep me around. If he liked me enough to kiss my hand, maybe I had a chance after all.

But I still doubted it.

When we entered the bedroom, it was nightfall. The stars appeared in the sky and could be seen through the open window. I hoped Crewe didn't have plans for the night. There was a lock on the door, and I doubted Dunbar would go out of his way to make me miserable, but I preferred it when Crewe was around.

He kept everyone in line.

He dropped his jacket and removed his watch, taking his time undressing in front of the closet. His tie came next then he unbuttoned his shirt.

I tried not to stare at him.

His physique was unlike anything I'd ever seen before. I'd never seen a man so hard and strong. He had lean muscles on a tall frame, his biceps leading to tight triceps. His pecs were so sculpted they didn't look real. He had a light tan line around his neck where his collared shirt ended, but it was so faint it was hardly noticeable. His shoulders were just as toned as the rest of him, packed with muscle but slender at the same time. The only time I'd ever seen a man look this beautiful was in porn, and that was all lighting and angles.

Crewe looked like that no matter what.

I swallowed when I realized my mouth was dry. I was a prisoner to a royal criminal, and I shouldn't feel anything but fear and disgust, but I found myself feeling so many contradicting emotions that none of it made sense.

His slacks and shoes came off next, and he stood in his black boxers.

I finally looked away, not wanting to get caught looking.

"I know you like what you see." He slowly walked toward where I sat on the couch. He had a noticeable V in his hips, lines caused by his tight abs. There was a distinct bulge in the front of his shorts, the outline of his long cock in the fabric.

"You shouldn't make assumptions."

He kneeled in front of me, his muscled mass coming into perfect view. He leaned in, one arm sitting on the armrest while the other touched my thigh. He looked at me with those light brown eyes, commanding me with just a look.

Now I couldn't turn away.

He leaned farther in until our lips were just inches apart. "Shallow breathing. Dry mouth." His hand squeezed the area just above my knee. "Quivering thighs." He grabbed my wrist next and felt my pulse. "Rapid heart rate."

I swallowed the shame as best I could.

He placed my hand over his chest, right over the skin where his heart was beating. "Rapid heart rate." He pressed his lips to my ear, his breaths falling on my earlobe. "Shallow breathing." He moved his mouth to mine and gave me a slow kiss. "Dry mouth." He grabbed my hand and forced my palm over his definition in his boxers. "Raging cock."

My hand automatically squeezed his length, my arousal making all the decisions for me. He was the biggest man I'd ever taken, but the painful stretching somehow felt incredible. I'd never been with a man like him before.

He leveled his face with mine. "Let's be real with each other. Tell me you want me."

I looked him in the eyes and didn't hesitate. "I want you."

His eyes became heavy-lidded, the answer obviously pleasing him. "I want you too." He kissed me and sucked my bottom lip into his mouth. "I don't want any other man to have you because I want you all to myself."

My hands moved into his hair, and I deepened the kiss, getting swept away by the arousal between my legs. He placed a transmitter inside my brother's brain, but that didn't stop me from wanting him. He kept me as his prisoner, but I still wanted to feel him between my legs. I hated this man, wished he were dead, but I still wanted to feel his come inside me.

Didn't make any sense.

Crewe lifted me from the couch and set me on the bed. His boxers were off, and his hard cock was already oozing at the tip.

I unbuttoned my jeans and shoved them off, eager to get him inside me.

He grinned in his typically arrogant way before he helped me get my panties off. He didn't bother with my shirt before he climbed on top of me and shoved himself deep inside my pussy. He was never gentle with me, fucking me like I didn't mean a damn thing to him.

But I liked it.

I had a dream I was walking down the road when a car sped by and slammed right into a tree.

I ran to the window to see if I could help whoever was behind the wheel, and I came face-to-face with my father. Eyes wide open with blood gushing down his face, he was already dead. My mother was in the passenger seat, a branch impaling her right through her stomach. I could smell the smoke from the engine and the blood from their wounds. In the back seat was Joey, a grown man as I last saw him. He was dead on impact. "Ahh!"

"London." Crewe's deep voice sounded in my ear, bringing me back to reality. "It's a dream. Wake up."

I kicked the sheets away like they were nets about to drag me underwater. Sweat was streaked up and down my arms and the backs of my thighs. I fought against an invisible foe, running from the car in my dream.

He grabbed me by both shoulders and shook me. "London, wake up."

I finally opened my eyes and saw the dark bedroom around me. I knew I was with Crewe, but I couldn't remember where. It was all a nightmare, a horrible dream that wasn't real. I jumped out of bed and felt the cold draft since I was naked. I ran to the fireplace then darted to the couch, moving so I wouldn't stand still. "Where am I?" This wasn't Scotland. This wasn't the island. I couldn't remember where I was. I was still asleep.

"Italy." Crewe got out of bed then slowly approached me, over six feet of pure man. "We came here to do business with Crow and Cane. You met them earlier today." He kept his voice low as if that might keep me calm.

I wrapped my arms around my body to hide my nakedness even though he'd already seen me. I backed farther into the chair and breathed deeply, trying to catch my breath and stop my frantically beating heart. No matter what I did, I couldn't calm down. My family's dead faces kept flashing before my eyes.

"I can't lose him…I can't." I burst into sobs, heavy sobs that made me shake.

"Lovely, whom? Can't lose whom?" He inched closer to me until his hand moved to my shoulder.

"Joey…he's all I have left." I covered my face with my palms and wept, my body shaking from the exertion. I didn't cry in front of people. I didn't cry at all. It didn't solve anything. It didn't make my problems go away. But I was out of my mind and still partially asleep.

Crewe wrapped his arms around me and pulled me into his chest, his strong arms acting as steel gates. His fingers moved into my hair, and he stroked me. "Shh…just a dream. Everything is alright."

I forced myself to stop crying, to stop feeling the violent emotions raging in my chest. With every single breath, I slowly calmed down until I was back to normal. The tears absorbed back into my skin, and I listened to Crewe's heartbeat for comfort.

It was just a nightmare.

A dream.

It'll be alright.

I had to talk myself through this hardship, but I was used to Joey being the one to console me. Even when I had a bad day in class, I called him and told him all about it. He wasn't just my brother. He was my whole family wrapped up into a single person. Without him, I was all alone. "I'm sorry…" I pulled away from Crewe, knowing I irritated him with my episode. He'd been woken up in the middle of the night with my tantrum, something he couldn't care less about. "Sometimes I have really vivid dreams if I drink too much…" I didn't want to see the anger in his eyes, so I didn't look at him.

He grabbed me by the elbow and guided me back into his chest. "It's alright, Lovely. I have nightmares too."

"You do?" Once my face was pressed against his chest again, I felt better. His heartbeat consoled me in a way I could never explain.

"All the time." He guided me to the bed and pulled the covers back so he could tuck me in. "You aren't alone."

My head hit the pillow, and he pulled the covers over me, tucking me in like a child.

He got into bed beside me, and instead of sticking to his side, he wrapped his arm around me and spooned me from behind. "You want to talk about it?"

My arm rested over his, gripping it like a lifeline. I could feel his pulse through his skin, the blood pounding away and giving him life. He was my captor, but he'd never made me feel more safe. It didn't make any sense. "No…"

He kissed the back of my neck before he rested his face against my hair. "I'm here if you change your mind."

I closed my eyes and felt sleep begin to take its toll. "I know."

I slept in late because of my rocky night.

Crewe was gone, probably already showered and ready for the day. He was usually awake as soon as the sun was up. He seemed to hit his private gym then got ready for the day. I knew he exercised because he wouldn't look like that unless he were committed.

I was relieved he was gone so I wouldn't have to face the humiliation right away. I had bad dreams from time to time, but nothing as intense as that. It felt like I was actually there, seeing the blood drip down their faces and seep into their clothes.

It was a dream I wanted to forget.

But the more terrifying the dream, the more difficult it was to block it out.

I wished I could call Joseph. He was the one person in the world I could talk to about this.

After I showered and got dressed, Crewe walked inside. He was already in his suit and tie, jumping into the workday. Instead of giving me his typical look of indifference, he stared at me like I was damaged goods.

Which I hated. "What are you up to today?" I didn't give him the chance to ask how I was feeling. I didn't want his concern, not after I'd embarrassed myself. When he held me, I should have pushed him away.

But I needed him too much.

"I'm heading down to the headquarters to meet with Crow and Cane. Just forgot my watch." He grabbed it off the dresser and fastened it around his wrist.

I was disappointed he was leaving. I would be stuck in this house with all of his men. As long as I didn't leave the room, they shouldn't bother me. I could wait to eat until he returned. "See you later." I didn't beg him to take me like I did yesterday. After the pathetic way I cried in his chest last night, I wasn't going to show an ounce of weakness again. It didn't look good on me.

It didn't look good on anyone.

He adjusted his cuff link as he looked at me. I'd never cared for brown eyes, but I loved his. They were warm like mocha but dark like the bark of a tree. They could be intense or playful at any given time. "Would you like to come with me?"

I froze in place because I couldn't believe he made the offer. After meeting with Crow and Cane yesterday, he was angry that he took me to begin with. Now he was asking on his own? It only took a few seconds for me to figure out why. "I'm okay. Thanks anyway."

He raised an eyebrow. "You don't want to come?"

"No. I'll stay here." I didn't mind pestering him until I got what I wanted, but the last thing I wanted was his pity. If he felt too terrible handing me off to Bones, that was one thing. But this was another.

He slid his hands into his pockets as he stared me down. "London."

I crossed my arms over my chest, refusing to give in. "Hmm?"

"I know you want to come, so what game are you playing?"

"I'm not playing any games. You're only inviting me because you feel bad for me. Don't feel bad for me. I hate that."

He glanced at his watch like he was running late. "I think having a pity party for yourself is worse than my feeling bad for you. But do whatever you want." He walked to the door with no intention of looking back.

I didn't want to be here alone, not when I had no idea how long he would be gone. I couldn't explore the property when Dunbar was giving me evil looks all the time. He was one of Crewe's trusted employees, but I knew he would betray Crewe if he thought he could get away with it. I could picture him holding me down and doing unspeakable things to me. And Ariel...she was a loose cannon. "Wait."

Crewe turned back around like he'd been expecting me to say something.

"I'll come with you."

He bottled his arrogance for once. "I'm leaving in five minutes. Hurry up."

It was just the two of us in his shiny black car. It was a two-seater, and judging by how loud the engine was, it was fast. I looked out the window and didn't ask him any questions. If I was lucky enough, last night wouldn't come up at all.

Crewe never had the radio on, which I thought was strange. He never listened to music.

"What are you doing with them today?"

"Going over weapon selection." He wore thick sunglasses, hiding his pretty eyes.

"Why did you buy weapons from them?"

"Protection is important. I want the best of the best."

"Do you have a lot of enemies?"

"Everyone has enemies. If you don't, then you're doing something wrong."

That was debatable. "I can stay in the car if you want…" He'd already done something nice by letting me come with him. I'd rather sit in a hot car than be back at the house with his men.

"Why do you hate Dunbar so much?"

"Because he's an ass. He's hit me twice now."

"He thought you were escaping."

I shook my head. "No. He has a problem with me. I honestly believe if you weren't around, he'd do something worse to me…just because he wants to."

Instead of shutting me down right away, Crewe considered what I said. "Dunbar has been working for me for a long time. He wouldn't cross me like that."

"I'm not so sure…"

"You need to give me more evidence than that."

"It's a gut instinct. I can just tell."

Crewe drove with one hand, his other arm on the windowsill. "I don't know about that."

"You've never been a woman. You don't know what it's like to feel like prey all the time. You wouldn't understand." I knew when a man wanted to cause me harm for his own sick pleasure. If Dunbar thought he could get away with it, he would force me on my stomach and take me like a dog.

Crewe turned to me, his gaze unreadable behind his glasses. He looked handsome in anything he wore, even sunglasses that hid some of his face from view. He could be wearing a sombrero and tights, and he would still look good. "I know what it's like to feel like prey. But no, I don't know what it's like to be a woman. You have me there."

I wondered if he was referring to his family's death. He was probably the last target on the list, but they never succeeded. "Do you think you could take me back to Fair Isle? I could be one of your women that you just see while you're there." He had women in Edinburgh, and probably everywhere else too.

"You like it there?"

"Yeah. I wouldn't be in your way, and I like Finley. Actually, he's the only employee you have that I feel comfortable with."

"When do you get in my way?"

He had a terrible memory. "It was just yesterday when you said how annoyed you were that you took me to see Crow and Cane."

"But you weren't in my way. And no, we aren't doing that."

I hid my disappointment as best as I could. "So, where you go, I go?"

"Exactly." He drove farther into the city and down a few streets until he reached a deserted complex. When he pulled up to the gate, the camera must have recognized his face because the doors opened and allowed him to pass through.

I searched the concrete complex and stared at the warehouses. It didn't seem like anything illegal was going on at first glance. "If I'm always around, how will you spend time with your other women?" I didn't like to think about him with anyone else. The fact that they were free and consensual just annoyed me. I'd give anything to have something consensual again. But I knew I was annoyed for other reasons too.

"I'll make it work." He killed the engine then got out.

I hid the sour look on my face before I got out and joined him.

Crewe took my hand and pulled me with him, keeping me right by his side as he moved. He entered the warehouse and greeted the men before he located Crow. His hand never left mine, and when he was face-to-face with the man we saw last night, his arm snaked around my waist. "Crow."

He nodded. "Crewe. Excited to see our inventory?"

"Impress me."

"This way." Crow guided us to a back room where we had privacy from the rest of the men. Cane was already there, placing the different guns on display. They were all black, military looking. Some were machine guns, and others were handheld pistols.

I felt a little nervous.

"They're unloaded." Crow smiled at me like he knew I was terrified.

Crewe kept me close to him as he examined everything. The only time he took his hand off my waist was when he used both hands to grab an AK-47. He felt the weight in his hands then aimed it at the opposite wall. He'd obviously handled guns before because it was clear he knew exactly what he was doing.

That made me uneasy. If I were back in New York, I'd be sitting in class right now, learning about the nervous system. But instead, I was in Italy with a man who intended to keep me and fuck me for as long as he wanted. He was examining a hoard of weapons he was about to buy from criminal masterminds.

How did Joey get mixed up in all of this?

"What do you think?" Cane asked. "Your woman seems impressed."

I shot him a glare.

Crewe didn't correct him. "Everything is well-made. You didn't cut corners."

"We never cut corners," Crow said. "You get what you pay for."

Crewe returned the gun to the table then moved on to a handgun. He felt the weight in his grasp then checked the barrel. It was empty like they claimed. He moved on and examined the different specimens, looking at minor details that I didn't notice with my untrained eye.

Crow turned his gaze on me, watching me like I might try something.

I stared back, threatening him with just my look.

The corner of his mouth rose in a smile, and he looked away. "Your woman has a backbone, Crewe. That's hard to find."

"She has a fist too," I said. "And she's not afraid to throw it in your face."

Crow grinned wider. "Don't let her go, man. She's a keeper."

Crewe grabbed another gun and examined it like he hadn't heard a word we said. "Everything looks good. Let's pack it up." He came back to my side, his thoughts still lingering on the weapons in the room.

"Of course it looks good," Cane said. "Fine Italian craftsmanship right here." Cane walked out of the room, probably to tell his men they needed to get everything together.

That left me with Crewe and Crow.

"How's Vanessa?" Crewe asked, probably to make conversation while we waited.

Crow's good mood immediately disappeared. He didn't turn angry, just dark and inhospitable. His green eyes looked darker, and his body stiffened noticeably with unease. Like a wild animal that had been provoked, his nostrils flared. "You know I'm in the middle of a war. And she's the leverage."

"What does that mean?" Crewe asked quietly.

I listened intently, knowing whatever Crow had to say was important.

"Bones took her. I've offered every asset I possess, and he still won't return her." Crow stared at the wall without blinking, his thoughts elsewhere. His body was absolutely still because he wasn't breathing. "I'll get her back…somehow."

I bowed my head so I could hide my face. I knew exactly who Bones was. I'd seen him in the flesh, seen the despicable look in his eyes. He was pure evil, disgusting and satanic. I tried not to shiver at the thought of what my life could have been. Whoever Vanessa was, she had the fate that I was almost destined for.

"I'm sorry." Crewe never apologized, and he seemed to mean it.

I wondered who Vanessa was. Was it Crow's wife? A girlfriend?

"Your sister doesn't deserve that." Crewe answered my unspoken question.

His sister? That was terrible.

Crow ran his hands through his hair, cringing like he was trying not to think about it. "It's been rough on both of us...can't sleep." He crossed his arms over his chest and stared at the floor.

I felt bad for being there, like I was intruding on something very personal.

I wondered if Crewe was going to mention that he'd recently seen Bones. It didn't seem like Crewe and Bones were friends, but they obviously had a working relationship. It made me wonder if Bones took Vanessa because he couldn't have me.

Was I directly responsible for this?

"Have you seen Bones lately?" Crow asked the question without warning, his eyes moving up to meet Crewe's gaze.

I wondered what Crewe would say.

"A few months ago."

Crow continued to stare at him with a poker face. "Were you doing business with him?"

"Sorta," Crewe answered before he glanced at me. "I was going to sell London to him…until I changed my mind."

Crow's eyes shifted to mine. "You're a lucky girl."

Sadly, I actually did feel lucky. I would much rather be Crewe's prisoner than anyone else's in the world. He was honest and transparent. He didn't get off on strangling me or cutting me. Plus, he was handsome and charming. The more I got to know him, the more I understood his personality. He'd been betrayed more than once—so he was cold. I wasn't justifying his actions. I just understood them.

"Is there anything I can do to help?" Crewe asked.

"I'm having a hard time tracking him down, getting him with his guard down," Crow answered. "When he leaves his premises, he rarely takes Vanessa with him. I'd have to get the two of them alone somewhere."

"What are you asking me?" Crewe asked.

"Is there a way you could get him somewhere alone with Vanessa?" Crow asked. "I'd be eternally grateful. Your purchase would be on the house, as a thank you."

I wasn't sure if Crewe would go for it. He wasn't the most charitable person in the world. "I don't want to get on his bad side. He's a good business partner and ally."

Crow nodded. "I've been feuding with him my whole life. He's not an enemy you want to have."

"Though, I'm willing to try something to make this work for you," Crewe said. "But I can't look guilty."

Crow nodded. "I understand."

"I'm celebrating the grand opening of my new distillery in Scotland. I can invite him. It wouldn't be suspicious." Crewe had his hands in his pockets, standing the same height as Crow. Both men were dark and mysterious, dangerously handsome.

I didn't want to be in the same room as that man—ever again. He made my blood turn cold and freeze over. Even though I belonged to Crewe, I didn't want to breathe the same air as that fiend, Bones. Knowing what he was doing to that innocent woman made me want to bash a goblet over his head.

"That could work," Crow said. "But I'm not sure if he'll bring her."

"I could suggest he bring a date," Crewe said. "But that's the most I can do."

Crow considered it before he nodded. "I'll take it. Thank you." He extended his hand. "Truly."

Crewe took it. "I had nothing to do with this, alright?"

Crow nodded. "Understood. Your weapons are on the house."

"That's not necessary," Crewe said. "If everything goes to plan, you can reimburse me. I can't guarantee he'll even come."

"That's true," Crow said. "We'll see what happens."

I didn't say anything on the drive home because I was at a loss for words. I had complained about my captivity with Crewe, but it could have been much worse. Whether he had a change of heart or truly thought keeping me with him was a better revenge, I was lucky I ended up in the passenger seat of his car.

Poor Vanessa.

Crewe broke the silence after a few minutes. "You alright?"

"No." I rested my hands in my lap and looked out the window.

"What's on your mind?"

"You already know." Ariel didn't care that I was a prisoner, but I cared that Vanessa had taken my place. No woman should be subjected to that kind of torture. My imprisonment wasn't fair either, but I could handle it.

"It's unfortunate." That was all he said about it, and he didn't seem to care.

"That was nice of you to help Crow." Maybe Crewe had a heart inside that tin chest after all.

"I'm sympathetic when it comes to family matters."

I guessed that shouldn't have been surprising after what happened to his own family. He was the last member of his line. Until he grew his own family, he would be alone.

"You're still putting your neck on the line. I respect you for it." Respect was something I hardly gave him, not when he manipulated me by threatening my brother. But his offer of help gave me hope that he was a good man after all, if he forgot about all his bitterness.

He kept his eyes on the road, his hand on the wheel.

I shouldn't have expected a response from that, but I got my hopes up anyway. "If Bones had taken me, do you think Vanessa would have been left alone?"

"I have no idea. He took her out of vengeance, so having you may not have made a difference. He could have gotten bored of you right away and killed you. Who knows?" He said it nonchalantly like my murder had no significance.

"Wow…he really is evil."

"They call him Bones for a reason."

I didn't want to know why, so I didn't ask. I looked out the window again. "When is this party?"

"Two weeks from Saturday."

I hoped he wasn't going to take me as his date. He took me the Holyrood thing, which was pretty high-profile. But maybe he would take his French diplomat or whatever. The idea of him taking someone else bothered me, but I refused to admit it—especially to myself. "In Scotland?"

"Yeah. The distillery is in Edinburgh."

"That's nice…" I wanted to ask if he was taking me, but I didn't want to bring it up.

"Are you ready to talk about last night?"

I thought that was buried. "No."

"Too soon?"

"No. I never want to talk about last night."

He drove down the country road, passing small houses with acres of land and crops. It was a cloudless day, and the sky was a clear blue. The sun shone through the window and hit both of my thighs, making them feel warm. "We're going to be together for a long time. You may as well make the best of it."

"Make the best of it?" I asked incredulously.

"Yeah. I could be your friend if you gave me a chance."

"Sorry, I'm not friends with criminals."

He smiled like he had a comeback sitting in the back of his throat. "But you're related to one?"

That jab hurt. "I didn't have a clue, and you know that."

"But you still love the guy, right?"

"Of course." I was offended by the question.

"Even though he breaks the law every single day?" he asked. "Even though he kills people?"

"He doesn't kill people," I said defensively. I purposely looked out the window to avoid his gaze. In reality, I really had no idea what Joseph's criminal activities included. All I knew was he stole intelligence from Crewe and tried to not pay for it. He tried to cheat a man out of four million dollars. That was the extent of my knowledge.

"And you know this, how?"

I didn't. "I don't want to talk about this anymore."

"Too bad," he said. "Your only relative lied to you. He got into a bad business even though he knew you could be used against him. He did it anyway. Me, on the other hand, I'm always honest. You're gonna get the truth from me even if you don't want to hear it. I'm the most trustworthy guy on the planet. You can always depend on me to deliver my promises. I'm a pretty powerful ally to have, Lovely. You should take advantage of that."

He must have struck a nerve because I suddenly felt lonely. I took his words to heart because I knew they were true. I even said them myself. Crewe was the only man in the world powerful enough to protect me. Only if he allowed me to leave would I escape. If he didn't let me go, I should make the best of the situation.

"So talk to me."

"Why do you care?"

He turned on another country road, his thick tires blowing up dust from the side of the road. The engine roared to life as he hit the gas and got back up to top speed. "Because I care about you."

"We have different definitions of the word."

"You're like a pet, Lovely. I want to take care of you so you'll last a long time."

So I was just a toy in his eyes. "I'm gonna get old and wrinkly one day."

He turned to me and winked. "You'll still be pretty damn hot. I can tell."

I rolled my eyes and ignored the charming comment. I knew he would be a good-looking older man. He had all the right features to stay beautiful. When he was older, he might even be sexier.

"So, tell me about your dream last night."

He was going to apply pressure until I broke. Since he was the only person in the world I socialized with, I was at his mercy. If I hadn't had him for companionship, I would have gone crazy months ago. "This a two-way street."

"No, it's not."

"Then it needs to be a two-way street. If you want my friendship, you have to give me yours. That's how it works."

He focused on the road like he was considering what I was saying. "Interesting arrangement."

"Wow. You must not have any friends if the concept is foreign to you."

"I don't," he said simply. "Looks like you'll be my first."

I was the prisoner, but I actually felt bad for him.

"How does this friendship thing work?"

"Friends are always honest with each other."

"Done," he said quickly. "That's easy."

"They trust each other."

"Hmm…I'm not sure I trust you not to kill me just yet."

If I could get away with it, I probably would. "As long as you have that transmitter, I'm at your mercy."

"True. And you know you can trust me?"

"In what way?"

"My intentions are always clear. I'll never surprise you. What else?"

"That's about it…other than genuinely liking each other."

"Well, I know I like you." He winked again. "What's not to like?"

"And I…don't absolutely despise you." That was the best I could do.

He grinned. "Wow. We're really making progress here." His hand moved to my thigh, and he gave it a squeeze. "I think that's the nicest compliment you've ever given me."

"Don't get used to it."

"So tell me about your dream."

"I'll tell you if you tell me what happened with Josephine."

He turned to me with his eyebrow raised. "What makes you think I'm gonna share that with you?"

"We're friends. That's what friends do. I tell you something, and you tell me something."

He shook his head. "I'm not telling you that."

"Why not?"

"It's none of your concern. That's why. Ask me something else." His foul mood suggested I shouldn't push any further.

"What's your favorite kind of ice cream?"

He looked at me like that was a stupid question. "Is that really your question?"

"It doesn't seem like you'll answer anything more personal…"

When he realized I was being serious, he answered. "I'm not a big fan of ice cream, but if I were going to choose, it would be chocolate."

"Wow. I feel like we're best friends already."

He chuckled then turned right again. In the distance was his villa, sitting on a small hillside with tall trees surrounding it. "Tell me about last night."

Like I was wearing an old bandage, I decided to rip it off. "I dreamt I saw the accident that killed my parents. But this time, Joey was in the back seat." I'd already cried last night, so I didn't have any emotion left. I said everything simply, like it didn't really matter. "I saw all the blood… their lifeless eyes. It felt real. I think that's why I got so upset." I looked out the window as we pulled up to the house, avoiding his gaze as much as possible. I wasn't embarrassed by my feelings, but I knew he didn't care about the way I felt. He probably just wanted to know because he was curious.

He pulled up to the driveway but didn't get out to hand his keys over to one of his men. He kept the car running, our faces hidden behind the tinted windows. He reached over and grabbed my hand, his long fingers warm and comfortable. Once his fingers were wrapped around mine, I felt better. He had pronounced knuckles, masculine hands that handled my feminine curves with ease. His hands hinted at his strength, the power he possessed from a lifetime of wealth. He had the ability to move mountains, to make a queen blush. No matter how much I hated him, I respected his majesty. No other man in the world had the kind of influence he did. "I have dreams like that, wondering how my parents suffered before they died. I have dreams of my brother as a man, how he would have aged if he'd lived. They come and go. Some nights are worse than others."

At least he understood.

One of his men approached the car but didn't open the door. He purposely waited for his employer to make the first move. Crewe glanced at him before he took off his glasses and set them on the dashboard. "I want to say it gets easier as time goes on. But it never does. It's been over twenty years, and I still haven't made my peace with it."

"How could you, when your family was murdered?" My parents were killed by a drunk driver, but it was unintentional manslaughter. The drunk driver didn't have a vendetta against my parents.

"Even after I kill the man who was responsible for this, I'll never find peace. I've accepted it. I'll always look over my shoulder everywhere I go. I'll always sleep with one eye open. I'll carry on my family name without them, but I'll never forget where I got my surname."

I turned my hand in his grasp so I could feel our palms rub together. My fingers caressed his, and I could feel the dry calluses that marked his hands. I never noticed them against my tits because I was too focused on what we were doing together. "Looks like we have a lot in common."

"We do. And I don't believe in coincidences."

"Does that mean you believe in fate?"

He stared at our joined hands before he looked at me. His eyes were impenetrable, impossible to decipher. "I believe what I see. And right now, I see you."

***

He sat on the balcony with the phone glued to his ear for a few hours. It didn't matter what country he was in, work never stopped. Ariel probably did a lot of work herself, but there were things Crewe had to attend to on his own.

I stayed in the bedroom and watched TV even though everything was in Italian.

He finally hung up the phone and walked inside, wearing his slacks and a collared shirt. His tie was loose and uneven.

I looked at him when I felt his commanding gaze.

"I have one more phone call to make."

I already knew what demand he was going to make. I'd seen that look on his face enough times to know what was coming next. Now that he had complete power over me, he could pull my strings like a puppet.

"I want you naked on your back, legs spread. I want you to touch yourself until I'm done—and think of me." When he came closer, I noticed the bulge in the front of his slacks. His fingers moved under my chin, and he grabbed me with restrained force. "Understand?"

I knew what response he was looking for. I knew what kind of mood he was in. "Yes, sir."

He dropped his hand and walked back outside. He shut the door then pulled out his phone for the last call of the day.

I swallowed the lump in my throat because my mouth was suddenly dry. Goose bumps marked my arms, but it wasn't because I was cold. Instead of being repulsed by the arrogant way he bossed me around, I was aroused.

I wanted him to go down on me.

He'd done it before, and it was the most amazing experience I'd ever felt. No man had ever made me feel that good, even the ones I thought I loved. But I didn't want to ask for it. It wasn't like I had any right to. That wasn't how our arrangement worked.

I did as he asked and got on the bed, my thighs spread apart. I'd touched myself before, but not because a man asked me to. He was going to walk in at any moment, and he would know if I'd followed directions or not.

My hand moved between my legs, and I rubbed my clit, picturing his mouth there instead of my fingers. My breathing slowly increased, my nipples hardened, and my eyes closed as I got into it. I moved my hand in a circular motion and arched my back as I pictured his mouth down below. In the beginning, I was self-conscious, but the more aroused I became, the less I cared how I looked. I doubted I looked sexy. At this angle, my appearance probably wasn't flattering.

When I heard something hit the floor, my eyes flashed open.

Crewe had already dropped his tie and shirt. Now his slacks were gone, and he stood in his boxers. His eyes smoldered as they took me in, the heat flushed across his face. He'd been watching me, but I had no idea for how long.

My hand stopped, and I suddenly felt embarrassed.

He grabbed his boxers and pulled them down. "Keep going, Lovely. Don't let me interrupt."

My hand moved again, and I stared at his long cock, suddenly hotter than I was before. He was the biggest and thickest I'd ever taken, and I wanted him now. It didn't matter who he was or that I hated him. I wanted this man more than any other.

He moved up the bed until he was suspended over me, my thighs still wide apart. He watched me with arousal in his mocha eyes, just as turned on as I was. His head was oozing from the tip. "You're the sexiest thing I've ever seen, you know that?"

My free hand wrapped around his neck, and I pulled him in for a kiss, wanting to feel his mouth against mine. The second we touched, I felt the jolt of pleasure rush through me. I rubbed my clit harder, getting swept away in the passion he elicited.

He kissed me back just as hard, breathing into my mouth.

"You're the sexiest man I've ever seen," I said against his mouth. I didn't think before I spoke. My hormones were doing all the thinking for me. My job was to make him fall for me, and flattery might be the way to do it.

He paused our embrace to look me in the eye, satisfied by my response. He kissed me again before he pulled my hand from between my legs. He pressed a small kiss to my fingertips before he placed them in his mouth and sucked.

My thighs squeezed around his hips automatically, my nipples hardening at the same time.

He sucked the taste of my pussy from my fingers before he pulled his mouth away. "Lovely, what were you thinking about?"

I knew exactly what that question meant. "You."

"And what was I doing?"

I was embarrassed to say the truth, even though I couldn't embarrass myself more. He'd already seen the worst of it. Instead of answering him, I kissed him again. Maybe that would be enough to get right to the point.

But he was too stubborn for that. He pulled away. "Tell me." He kissed the corner of my mouth and pressed his fingers against my clit. He rubbed me aggressively, touching me better than I touched myself.

When he made me feel so good, I couldn't think straight. "You went down on me."

His fingers slowed, and he gave me one final kiss. He trailed kisses down my body until he reached the apex of my thighs. He scooted down until he was on his stomach below me, his face between my legs.

I immediately writhed, my fingers digging into his hair. "God...yes." My nails moved into his shoulders, and I nearly sliced the skin. My hips flexed, and I pressed myself farther into his mouth. I wanted every inch of his tongue against my clit. I wanted it inside of me, outside of me. With this blinding pleasure, I couldn't think about anything other than how good he felt, of getting more of him. "Crewe…" His name shouldn't have left my lips, not when it increased his power over me, but I didn't care in the moment.

He blew on my slit before he circled his tongue around my clit again, applying more pressure until he hit me in the perfect spot. He made me come violently, sending me over the edge when I didn't realize I was standing on the cliff face to begin with.

"Crewe…" My head rolled back, and I closed my eyes, enjoying the sensual fire that ripped through me. It was powerful, incredible. It was of the best orgasms he'd ever given me, the kind that made my pussy clench even when he wasn't inside me. I pooled at my entrance, and Crewe licked it away like he wanted every drop.

After the climax subsided, it slowly faded away. The tenderness between my legs throbbed even when the ecstasy was gone, so every touch of his tongue still made my hips jerk with pleasure.

He lifted his head and raised himself up, a gleam of moisture coating his lips. His cock twitched with arousal as he moved himself on top of me. His skin was flushed with blood where his muscles flexed and worked to hold himself up, and a thin line of sweat formed over his pecs and neck. I wished I weren't so attracted to him, but there was no way my body could ignore how incredible he was. Not only was his body awe-inspiring, but he had a rugged jawline and warm, mocha eyes.

Instead of remaining satisfied, I wanted more. I wanted his thick cock inside me, to stretch me deep and wide like every man should stretch his woman. I gripped his biceps and guided him farther on top of me. "Fuck me now."

A quiet growl escaped his lips, and his eyes hardened. He widened my legs and pinned his arms behind my knees, adjusting my hips and stretching my lower back in a way he never had before. He bent me exactly the way he wanted me and pressed his head to my entrance. Slowly, he sank into me.

Somehow, that felt more incredible than his face pressed between my legs. "Crewe…"

"Fuck, that is some wet pussy."

"Because you make me wet."

He stopped sliding into me and stared at me with his smoldering expression. "Lovely…Jesus Christ." He sank the rest of the way, inserting his entire length until his balls hit my ass.

My nails dug into his triceps, feeling the solid muscle that was tighter than a rope.

He didn't rock into me slowly like the other times we'd had sex. He pounded into me hard right from the beginning, tapping the headboard against the wall with the velocity of his thrusts. He breathed hard through the exertion, his powerful body becoming coated with sweat within minutes.

My hands dragged down his chest, and I felt my tits shake as he fucked me hard. I loved watching his face as he moved inside me, the sexy clench of his jaw and the hard look in his eyes. Sweat formed at his temples and a drop splashed onto my chest. I loved watching him fuck me as hard as he could, taking me roughly as if he couldn't bear to have me any other way.

I was gonna come again. I could feel it deep inside my pussy where he was hitting me. Like there was a special button inside me, he pushed the trigger. My hands moved up the back of his neck, and I gripped his hair, holding on to him as an anchor while the fire swept through my body. "Crewe…I'm coming."

He breathed hard through his thrusts. "I know." He pumped into me harder, grinding against my clit and giving me an extra push for a more powerful orgasm than before. I spiraled into a chaotic whirlwind of satisfaction and screamed through the sensation, not caring if everyone in the house heard me.

"Give it to me…" My hands slipped through his sweat as I tried to grab on to him.

He closed his eyes and released an involuntary moan before his thrusts ceased. He inserted himself completely inside me before he came, his cock thickening within me as he released. Another violent moan escaped his mouth again as he finished, filling me with every ounce of his seed.

Now that the fun was over, I lay back and caught my breath. I didn't realize how sweaty I was until we were both satisfied. My body had been moving with his the entire time, my body meeting his thrusts as I took his length when he gave it. I didn't even realize it was happening. When Crewe and I fucked, I didn't think about anything else but our bodies moving together.

And I suspected he didn't either.

CREWE

When we were finished, London got into the shower.

She walked away without speaking a word, her hair stuck to the sweat on her neck. When she walked away, some of my come seeped from her entrance and down the inside of her thigh. I watched it trail down until she was no longer in the room.

Fuck, that was hot.

I lay back on the bed and listened to the shower run. Her naked body was under that warm water, her smooth skin wet and slippery. My body was covered in sweat, and I didn't want to lie on the bed anymore.

I decided to join her.

She stood under the water with shampoo massaged into her hair. The soap bubbles clung to various parts of her body, including her tits. Her curves were even more beautiful surrounded by a cloud of steam.

She didn't turn around when I walked inside, either because she didn't care or didn't notice. The shower was large, big enough for more than two people, so I wasn't hogging her space.

I was satisfied with that erotic session, but I wanted to be with her anyway. I'd counted the number of times she said my name.

Four.

Maybe she hated me. Maybe she wished I were dead. But she certainly enjoyed fucking me.

That gave me a strong sense of accomplishment.

I'd never forget the sight of her touching herself, getting her pussy wet by thinking about me. She didn't even notice that I'd walked into the room because she was lost in the moment, her nipples hard and her breathing deep and ragged. Her thighs were spread wide, and she rubbed that wet clit with everything she had.

When my mouth pressed against her lips, I knew how soaked she was.

Drenched.

She went crazy when I went down on her. Her nails nearly cut me because she gripped me so tightly. She flexed her hips and gave me more of herself, and that only made me want more of her.

She was incredible.

I'd never had sex as amazing as that. I'd never been with a woman so gorgeous. I knew she was my slave and had no way of escape, but that wasn't an act. She enjoyed me.

Every. Fucking. Inch.

I pressed my chest to her back and wrapped my arms around her petite waist. My mouth found her shoulder, and I pressed a kiss there, tasting the soap she'd just lathered into her body. I preferred to taste my own sweat on her body, but this would do.

She turned her head over her shoulder. "Wanted to keep me company?"

Wanted to keep myself company. "No. Just wanted to save water." My hands slid across her waist and back to my sides.

"Very noble." She turned around and tilted her head back so she could rinse the shampoo out of her hair. Her tits were soapy and wet, curvy and flawless. She had the perfect body, and it didn't seem like she even realized it.

I grabbed the shampoo bottle and squirted some into my hair. I lathered the soap as I watched her stand under the shower, the suds running down her body. She was in a different mood when she was satisfied. Like rose petals on the wind, she drifted slowly. With lidded eyes, she was calm and peaceful.

It was the direct opposite of how she was just minutes ago.

She was a good lay the first time I had her, but the more we were together, the more her colors showed. We knew each other's bodies better, understood each other's likes and dislikes. I'd never bedded the same woman so frequently besides Josephine, and that didn't even count. Our relationship was short and rushed. That's probably why it didn't last long. And Josephine wasn't even that great in the sack. London, on the other hand, was incredible. I wonder if her list of partners was as long as mine.

I never wondered if she left anyone behind. Was she seeing someone when my men snatched her from her bed? Did she have a boyfriend looking for her? Or was she promiscuous like I was, hopping from man to man?

The idea of her being with a bunch of guys suddenly made me angry. It had nothing to do with her lifestyle choice. I just didn't like picturing other men inside her. Must be because I owned her. Now that she was my property, I was annoyed that she ever belonged to anyone else.

Man, I was a psychopath.

How could I be irritated with anything she did before I stole her? "Did you leave anyone behind before you joined me in Scotland?" I worded it in a much more appropriate way than I wanted to.

"I told you Joseph is my only family member. I had some friends, but that was about it."

She didn't understand my question. "Did you leave a man behind?" If I looked at her social media account, would it say she was in a relationship? Was some nice guy crying over her every night while I fucked her? If that was the case, it didn't seem like she was thinking about him when I was inside her.

"A man?" She pumped conditioner into her hand before she massaged the ends of her strands. "No. I didn't leave a man behind."

The irritation in my chest disappeared. If she did have a man, I would look at her differently. I would feel like I was sharing her with someone who wasn't even there. I moved under the water and rinsed my hair, wearing a mask so she didn't know what I was thinking. "Been with a lot of guys?"

She did a double take, clearly offended by what I just asked. "Excuse me?"

That came out wrong. I didn't word that very well. I was just so eager for an answer that I didn't think it through. "That came out wrong."

"You bet your ass that came out wrong."

I wanted to smile at her feistiness. If she hadn't stood up for herself at that comment, I would think less of her. "You seem experienced. That's all I was getting at."

She continued to massage her hair with conditioner.

I wasn't getting anything out of her, and I didn't know how to get my answer. "Did you have any serious boyfriends?" That wasn't too invasive.

She ran her fingers through her hair and coated each strand with the moisture. She had a lot of hair, so it took her a while. "When have you ever beaten around the bush? If you want to know something, just ask."

My little spitfire. "How many men have you been with other than me?"

She stepped under the shower and tilted her head back. She ran her fingers through her hair as she counted in her head. "Four."

That's it? I was expecting a lot more than that. "Four?"

"Yeah. Why?"

I gave her an honest answer. "You're amazing in bed."

Her fingers paused in her hair for a moment before she continued to rinse. "It takes two to tango."

The corner of my lip rose in a smile. "I've been with a lot of women. I could have just laid there, and it still would have been spectacular."

She shrugged then wrapped her fingers around her hair before she squeezed the water out.

"Who were these four guys?"

"What does it matter? Are you going to tell me about every woman you've been with?"

"I will if you do."

"I don't care about all the women you've been with," she said coldly. "I'm sure you can't even remember them all."

Not true. "I remember every woman I sleep with. I have a lot of regulars in various places. It's not always about hooking up with a stranger before I continue on my way." I wasn't that cold. I gave them my attention and my respect—but nothing else.

"But I doubt they ever meant anything to you."

Only Josephine did before she stabbed me in the back. "What does it matter if they did or didn't?"

She closed her eyes as the water fell down her face. "I guess it doesn't."

"Tell me about these four guys."

She ran her hands over her hair then stepped out from under the water. "Why are you so interested?"

"Answer the question." It didn't matter why I was interested. I just wanted her to answer the damn question.

"The first guy was my high school sweetheart. It didn't last long, and we were both learning. The second one was my freshman year in college. Went to a party and met a cute guy…you know how that goes. The third guy was my junior year in college. We saw each other for a while. And the last one was from my first year of medical school. We saw each other casually because we were too busy studying."

Now that I had my answer, I was annoyed. But what did I expect to happen? There was no answer she could give that would make me feel better about the others before me.

"So I'm not very experienced," she said. "At least, not more than most."

It seemed like it.

She squeezed the water out of her hair again. "Is the interrogation over?"

I ignored the irritation in her voice. "Was never meant to be an interrogation."

"If you learned to talk to people the correct way, people would open up to you."

I didn't want to take the time to learn. I just wanted my answers immediately.

She left the shower running as she stepped out and grabbed a towel. Her ass was perky, and her thighs were toned. I wanted to trail my fingers up and down the back of her leg, to feel the smoothness of her skin. She patted her hair dry before she finished it with a blow-dryer and moisturized her skin.

I stayed in the shower and watched her discreetly, taking in every inch of her luscious curves. Her beauty captured my attention, but everything underneath her skin was more fascinating to me. Her feistiness never waned, and she always fought for self-respect even if I insulted her. Most of the women I dealt with were timid and shy. I could push them around all I wanted because they never stood up to me. Josephine was like that.

London never was.

That opposition should annoy me, but it didn't. I respected a woman who respected herself. I was aroused by the fire that constantly burned behind London's eyes. The only time she was compliant was when my commands turned sexual. She didn't have a problem following orders then.

Because she liked it.

The two of us had very little in common, but our chemistry was scorching. I liked the fact that she needed me once in a while. The rest of the time, she handled herself. She wasn't a damsel in distress. She barely needed me for anything.

It was a nice change.

Seeing Josephine crawl back to me and admit she made a mistake was a major turn-off. I never fantasized about her coming back to me, and I respected her less because of it. She traded in my love for royalty—because I wasn't good enough.

Fuck her.

If any man ever earned London's love, they must have truly deserved it. She wasn't easy to impress. There was nothing a man could give her that she couldn't give herself. Independent and strong, she was perfect. After she was captured, she still fought me tooth and nail. Anyone else would have sobbed all day and night, but she never shed a tear.

She was tough as steel.

———

Dunbar texted me. *We're ready for you, sir.*

I shoved my phone into my pocket and walked into the bedroom. London was sitting on the couch reading a book. She never watched TV or read the magazines my men brought for her. She had a very specific way of entertaining herself. "We're leaving."

She finished the paragraph she was reading before she gave me her attention. "For good?"

"Just for the afternoon. Come on." I was in my jeans and t-shirt today since I had no meetings. I hit my private gym and went for a run along the countryside road before London had woken up that morning.

"I'm not a dog." She snapped the book shut. "Where are we going?"

"Shopping. There's a Valentino studio in Florence."

"A Valentine what?"

I guess I shouldn't be surprised she didn't recognize designer clothing. She was too absorbed in school to care about fashion. "We need to get you a gown for the opening in a few weeks." I never had to repeat myself so many times with other people. Anytime London and I spoke, our arguments just went around and around.

"You're taking me to your distillery opening?" she asked in surprise.

"Yes. Now get your ass up so we can go."

She finally stood up. "Why are you taking me?"

"What kind of question is that?"

"I'm not good for this sort of thing."

"You did fine at the Holyrood celebration."

She raised an eyebrow. "I hardly said a word, and I stuck to your side the entire time. I wasn't much company."

"I like a quiet woman." I grinned because I knew that would piss her off.

And it did. "Interesting. I like a silent man."

I loved her comebacks. "I'm not taking you for your conversational skills. I'm taking you because you look absolutely gorgeous—clothed or unclothed."

The compliment didn't affect her like my other ones did. "Take someone else, Crewe. I don't want to go."

Both of my eyebrows rose at her disobedience. "I don't recall giving you a say in the matter." Did I need to pull out the transmitter and remind her what was at stake? That I could kill her brother with the press of my thumb?

"Look, I don't want to go. Take someone who would truly enjoy the evening and your company."

"I want to take you. That's final." I didn't want to hear another word out of her. My word was law. I always got my way—no matter what.

She crossed her arms over her chest and retained her angry look. "No."

Now she'd crossed a line. "Do I need to remind you that your brother's life is in my hands?" I inched closer to her, my jaw hard and my eyes unforgiving. I was tempted to grab her by the neck and throw her on the bed with her pants around her ankles. I wanted to spank her until her ass was blood red.

"I don't want to be in the same room as that psychopath." Her words escaped as a whisper, but her voice shook. She never showed fear to anyone, not even me. But the thought of Bones clearly made her uncomfortable, made her twist as if a knife had penetrated deep into her gut. "I don't want to look at him. I don't want him to look at me." She finally broke our eye contact and turned her gaze in a different direction, as if she were ashamed of the confession.

I didn't blame her for being so disturbed. He was so disgusting that I actually changed my mind about handing her over to him. When I'd pictured that chain around her neck as she cradled a broken arm, I'd turned soft. I didn't want that fate for her. I needed to make Joseph pay for what he did, but I couldn't waste such a perfect woman. She deserved better than that. This woman actually made me somewhat compassionate—which was an accomplishment. "He won't lay a hand on you. I promise."

"I still don't want to look at him." She stepped away as if she needed space. "I don't want to be in the same room as him. I don't want to breathe the same air. All I'll think about is the way he grabbed my tits and punched me... like I was some kind of animal." She turned around altogether, hiding her face.

I suspected tears had built up in her eyes. The only time I'd seen her cry was after her nightmare. She refused to show weakness to anyone, but she allowed me to catch glimpses. Her interaction with Bones was limited, but the three-day period she waited for him to retrieve her must have been just as scarring. She couldn't sleep or eat because she knew what her fate would be. That must have been the worst part.

I came behind her and rested my hands on her hips. My face pressed against the back of her head, my nose catching the smell of her freshly washed hair. She'd used my shampoo, but it didn't smell masculine on her. With her own scent, she made it flowery and sexy. I felt the slight but prominent curves of her frame with my fingertips and noticed the way she inhaled deeply the second I touched her. "You're always safe with me, Lovely. A man won't even look at you unless they have my explicit permission. You don't need to be afraid."

"You don't know what it's like to be prey..." She'd said that to me once before.

"They call me the scotch king for a reason. I own the industry, and soon I'll own the world. And as my queen, you don't need to be afraid of anyone. You're my possession, and no one will lay a hand on you. I promise."

She breathed again, feeling my hands glide up her torso. "But I'm not your queen. I'm just your slave…"

I pulled her against my chest and rested my chin on her head. "Either way, you're still untouchable." I'd wanted to make Josephine my queen, but being royal in scotch didn't mean anything to her. Now I needed the right woman for the spot. London couldn't be the woman for that. She didn't have the right blood, the right wealth. But she wasn't nothing either. "You can hold your head high and look him in the eye without fear, Lovely. I've never seen you bow before. Don't start now."

———

Jacques looked London up and down, his face a mask as he examined her. It was difficult to tell what he was thinking until he expressed his feelings candidly. His fingertips rested against his lips as he circled her, looking at her specific measurements and her qualities.

I was certain making her look beautiful would be easy.

I sat on the gray couch, and his assistant brought me an expensive bottle of wine and two glasses. I didn't care for wine, but I drank it to be polite. Some expensive brands of champagne were pleasing, mainly the ones with the highest alcohol content. I crossed my legs and watched London stand on the pedestal, her brown hair over one shoulder and body slumped with a lack of self-confidence. It was out of character for her to look that way, but she was being silently judged by a stranger.

After five minutes of silence, Jacques finally clapped his hands. "I've got it." He disappeared into the back where all the gowns were stored. I didn't know a lot about fashion, but I knew each dress was nearly one of a kind. They only made them in size zero to six, and even then, there were very few of them. Otherwise, all the rich people would be wearing exactly the same thing.

London looked at herself in the mirror, an unreadable expression on her face. Her eyes were lifeless, and her shoulders weren't straight. She still didn't want to attend this dinner with me, but she'd stopped arguing about it.

Jacques returned. "Here." He held a sweetheart-cut gown that was a mix of purple and pink fabric. Everything blended together well, having a slight shimmer that wasn't overpowering. I usually only paid attention to the kind of suits I preferred, but I knew that gown was extraordinary. "Put it on then come back out here and show it off."

London took it by the hanger, her eyes roaming over the fabric like she was studying it with genuine interest. She walked into the fitting room and shut the curtain.

Jacques walked over to me, dressed in black jeans and a black t-shirt. For a fashion expert, he wore the same drab outfit every time I saw him. It didn't express any presence. "That's one stunning girl."

Since he was gay, his comment didn't bother me. "I know."

"She's got the perfect cheekbones, the perfect eyes…that hourglass figure would look perfect on the runway. That dress is a little revealing for a fancy occasion, but I know she'll pull it off. The second she puts it on, she'll fall in love."

I imagined London was a jeans and t-shirt kind of woman. She didn't seem to care about my expensive cars or real estate. Her tastes were very singular, like fresh flowers in a vase or the sun breaking through the clouds on a cold winter day. She didn't want things. She just needed something meaningful. "Hopefully. She doesn't want to attend this party with me."

"Maybe the dress will change her mind."

London walked out a moment later and stepped onto the circular riser in the center of the room. The gown was the perfect height for her, and it fit her frame exactly the way Jacques predicted.

He clapped as he walked up behind her. "I knew it would be *magnifiqué*." He ran his fingers along the side. "This color is perfect for your skin tone. And your shoulders can totally pull this off." He walked around as he fluffed the gown, making her look like a model about to be photographed. He joined her on the stage then quickly threw up her hair, putting it in a cute braid before he pinned it up. "You've got to keep your hair out of your face for this one. You have such nice collarbones, a slender neck, a perfect bust size…" He stepped back and admired her. "Mr. Donoghue, you have to buy this gown for her. I insist."

I chuckled. "You're quite the salesman."

"This dress was made for her." He walked around her. "Look at her."

I knew she would look beautiful, but she really was breathtaking. I wanted to rip it off her and fuck her the way I did last night—with all that sweat and passion. She would steal the focus for my opening. People would forget why they were even there once they looked at her. "What do you think, Lovely?"

She stared at herself in the mirror then ran her fingers down the front. "It's beautiful."

"Then that's settled." Jacques clapped his hands once. "Take it off, and I'll wrap it up for you. You got a quite a deal, Mr. Donoghue. The price just dropped to ten thousand euro."

London did a double take. "This is a ten-thousand-dollar dress?"

For the first time, Jacques looked offended. "It's Valentino, girl. Worth every penny."

London shut her mouth, knowing anything else she said would get Jacques worked up. She left the platform and returned to the fitting room to get dressed.

Jacques was still flustered by her comment. "Some people don't understand quality."

I felt the need to defend her even though I shouldn't. "She comes from humble beginnings. I wouldn't worry about it."

"Well, it's time to drop the humility. If she's with you, she's a very rich woman."

London and I sat in the back of the car while Dunbar drove us back to the house. London was quiet, having nothing to say after her comment at the studio. Ever since I'd told her she would be my date for the evening, she'd closed like a clam.

I didn't care for it.

I hit the button on the ceiling and closed the divider between Dunbar and us.

London tensed, probably knowing what was coming.

"That dress looked stunning on you. I hope you like it."

Her legs were crossed, and she clung to the window like she was trying to get away from me. "It's gorgeous. I never thought something so expensive would hug my body."

"I've hugged your body plenty of times," I said with a smile.

She kept her gaze out the window. "I love it, but I don't care for the price. That's excessive, if you ask me."

"You get what you pay for."

"That dress couldn't have cost more than a few hundred dollars to make."

"That's not the point. Its value extends beyond the fabric. You'll get used to the finer things in life. Give it time."

"I'm not so sure…"

I didn't like this version of her, subdued and defeated. I wanted that fiery backbone, that no-bullshit attitude. I liked the warrior, not the conquered. "I hope the idea of Bones isn't still weighing you down."

"He's not…for the most part."

Now my interest was piqued. I shouldn't care about how she felt. Her emotions weren't my problem. She was there to service me, to do exactly what I asked without question. Her thoughts and opinions didn't matter.

But I still cared anyway. "What's on your mind?"

She watched the fields pass before she answered. "If I were back home right now, I'd either be studying for an exam or doing my nightly rounds at the hospital. I wouldn't be hanging out with friends or having a good time. My life would be centered around work. It would be drab and boring…but it would still be mine. Now I'm in Italy, buying an expensive gown and living in a mansion. I'm your prisoner simply because I'm related to your enemy. My favorite person in this new world is your butler. Everything has changed so much… I'm not sure how I feel about it."

I shouldn't pity her. Her sadness wasn't my problem. But I did pity her—a lot. "You know I can never let you go, Lovely. I know this is hard for you, but it's easier just to accept your fate and not think about the past."

She shook her head. "The worst part is…you're the only friend I have. Is it weird that I see you as a friend?"

I saw her in the same light. "Not at all."

"That I have sex with you and I like it."

"I like it too." My cock hardened in my slacks at her confession. There was nothing sexier than pleasing a woman who wanted to be pleased. She fucked me harder than I fucked her most of the time.

"That I feel safe with you."

"You should feel safe with me." I would never let anything happen to her unless I wanted it to happen. The only person who would ever end her life would be me. She didn't need to look over her shoulder in fear.

"That I'm actually grateful you didn't just kill Joseph once he betrayed you."

"You should feel grateful," I whispered. "I've been very merciful."

She rested her elbow on the windowsill and held her chin up with her fingertips. "I miss my old life, but I'm grateful you captured me. There are worse things than living with you…like being Bones's prisoner. And my brother can still be a free man. If I were offered the trade, I would have taken it in a heartbeat."

Did that have anything to do with me personally? "You're loyal. That's a rare thing to find."

"We're family," she whispered. "Now that I've met people like Dunbar and Bones, I know there are truly cruel men out there. You aren't one of them."

That offended me. "I am cruel, Lovely."

"You've never laid a hand on me."

"I've slapped you a few times." And I liked it.

"Because I was talking back or trying to run. You didn't punch me in the face with all your strength like Bones did."

Because I didn't find black eyes sexy.

"You feed me, clothe me, and you don't put chains around my neck. It could be much worse…that's all I'm saying."

"You're a very optimistic person." If it were me and there was no way to escape, I would have killed myself.

She shrugged.

"Or you actually like me."

She rolled her eyes. "You wish."

I grabbed her hand gently and pulled her against me, wanting her to lean against my hard chest rather than the windowsill. "I know you like me."

"I tolerate you. Big difference."

"I don't buy that."

"Well, you should."

I grabbed her chin and turned her face toward mine. Her plump lips looked kissable, coated with a thin layer of moisture from her saliva. Her eyes became lidded, prepared for the kiss before I even leaned in. I could feel the shiver through her body, or perhaps I just imagined it because I felt it. I leaned in and pressed a kiss to her mouth, not surprised to feel her kiss me back. She always met my passion with her own. She was an incredible kisser, a perfect partner. My tongue dived into her mouth, and I met hers as they danced together. She didn't kiss me so well because she hated me. She kissed me like that because she enjoyed me as much as I enjoyed her. I pulled away when I'd proved my point. "Like I said, I don't buy that."

5

LONDON

We headed back to Scotland in Crewe's private jet along with the rest of his team.

Including Ariel.

She sat on the opposite side of the aisle with her laptop out. We had a mutual understanding to pretend neither one of us existed at any given moment of time.

Crewe remembered my fear of flying because he grabbed my hand the second we sat down and held it through takeoff. He talked to me about Italy to get my mind off the terrifying ordeal and even succeeded in keeping me calm.

My fear of flying was irrational. I needed to forget about it and just move on.

Crewe made that a lot easier when he was sweet to me. His moments of tenderness had become more frequent. He held me through my nightmare, listened to my fears with sympathy, and when I told him I was scared, he always assured me I would be safe.

He didn't look like a monster anymore.

That's when I knew I needed to make a change.

I had to get out of here.

As if I had Stockholm syndrome, I had been brainwashed. I found my captor compassionate and understanding, but in reality, he was keeping me against my will. I shouldn't feel grateful toward him for anything. He was preferable to Bones, but maybe he was never going to give me to Bones in the first place. Maybe that was all a stunt to coerce me into appreciating him.

The fact that I liked Crewe, enjoyed fucking him and spending time with him, was a huge warning sign. I should be exactly how I used to be when I was fighting him every chance I had. The fact that I'd softened so much, leaned on him for support, told me I was going crazy.

I had to get out.

I thought about the last thing Joseph said to me, over and over. It filled my thoughts during the entire plane ride. Crewe had a few glasses of scotch then fell asleep with his head against the leather chair. He didn't shave that morning before we left, so a thick beard was beginning to come in. He was just as handsome asleep as he was awake.

I could feel the stirring in my belly when I felt the sizzle of attraction.

I wanted to kiss him.

That was ludicrous. The only thing I should want to do was murder him.

Joseph's plan was the only thing I had at my disposal at the moment. I would never be free again unless I got inside Crewe's head. If I made him fall for me, made him love me, I could get him to let me go. Or I could get him to allow me to escape without repercussion. If I didn't do something, this would be my life.

His slave.

I would travel all over with him and keep him company. Some nights he would be with his other whores. Then he would come back to me once he was finished with their entertainment. He would marry someone suitable, have children, and I would still be the woman on the side when he wasn't interested in his wife.

I would never get married.

Have my own children.

Practice medicine.

I would never have the freedom to make my own decisions.

All of it hit me hard in the chest and made it difficult to breathe. All of my rights had been taken away, and I would never know the life I was meant to have. And worst of all, I was slowly beginning to care for Crewe.

To get jealous when he was with other women.

To miss him when he wasn't around.

To need him to sleep with me every night.

How did this happen?

I had to end it now. I had to get him exactly where I wanted him.

I had to become his queen.

The castle was just as majestic as it'd been when we left. With stone walls that were impenetrable and courtyards full of roses and hydrangeas, it was an historical masterpiece. I loved the house in Italy, but I preferred the ancient halls of Scotland. I didn't explore much of it last time I was here, but perhaps Crewe would allow me to wander.

The men carried our bags upstairs into the royal chambers, and Crewe got into the shower.

I'd thought about my plan through the entire flight, but I hadn't come up with a proper way to execute it. I'd never gotten a man to fall in love with me before. I didn't know how to be sexy. I didn't know how to be what Crewe was looking for.

I knew he liked sex.

I knew he liked it when I needed him.

I knew he liked seeing me in that gown.

If I could focus on those things, maybe I could pull it off.

I undressed and joined him in the shower. His six-foot-two frame was lean and carved with muscle. He had flawless skin that was dotted with a freckle here and there. Every time he moved his arms, I could see the muscles shift underneath the skin. He was powerful and beautiful at the same time.

I came up behind him and pressed a kiss to the center of his shoulder blades. "Do you mind if I join you?"

He rubbed a bar of soap across his chest and returned it to the tile shelf. "Never."

I circled my arms around his waist and felt the soap against my fingertips. "Thanks for making me feel better on the plane…"

His arm moved over mine. "Of course, Lovely." He turned and faced me, his facial hair still thick because he hadn't shaved. He usually did that after he got out of the shower, when his skin was moist and soft. His arms moved around my waist, and he stared at my breasts with a heated gaze.

I needed to be sexy. I needed to be different from the other women he'd been with. I needed to give him whatever he wanted. I put aside all my self-consciousness and grabbed my tits with my hands. Slowly, I began to massage them, my thumbs swiping over my nipples. I grabbed some of the soap from his chest then spread it down the valley between my breasts.

Crewe watched every move I made.

I felt silly in the beginning, but when I saw the scorching look in his eyes, I didn't feel so stupid. My nipples hardened because I became aroused. No man had ever made me feel more desirable. It was obvious how much he wanted me, and a man had never shown me such a profound level of sexual interest. I was asked out on dates. Men tried to pick me up in bars. But I never got a look like the kind Crewe was giving me right now.

His cock hardened against his stomach the longer he watched me. Nine inches emerged out of nowhere, hot, circulating blood filling his shaft.

I continued to grope myself before I licked my lips.

Crewe moaned loudly enough that I could hear it over the running water.

I took it a step further and lowered myself to my knees. The bathroom tile was hard and uncomfortable against my knees, but my unease would feed his desire even more. I kept my hands on my tits then opened my mouth, my tongue flattened and ready to go.

Crewe's eyes darkened, and he grabbed his base, getting ready to shove it into my mouth. The last time I sucked his dick was because he commanded it. Now I was doing it willingly, prepared to be choked for his pleasure.

I looked up at him with my tongue sticking out, silently asking for his cock.

"Fuck…" He grabbed the back of my head and slowly inserted his length across my tongue. He aimed his cock then moved inside. His fingers dug into my scalp as he stood tall above me, conquering me.

I felt his tip hit the back of my throat, but I didn't allow myself to gag. I could taste him immediately, soap mixed with his arousal. I craned my neck and took his length over and over, taking my time so I could get used to the fullness in my throat.

I played with my tits again as I moved, licking his base to the tip and then down again.

He closed his eyes for a second as he enjoyed it, his fingers moving to my shoulder for balance.

I moved quicker, wanting to give him more. But the more I moved, the more I enjoyed it. I liked the way tears pooled in my eyes because he was so big. I loved the way my throat hurt because he was so long. I loved the way he continued to ooze in my mouth with pre-come. I loved the way his desire burned in his eyes as he wanted more of me.

This was supposed to be for him, pure manipulation. But I found myself enjoying it just as much.

"Look at me."

My gaze moved up to his eyes as I kept going.

His large hand cupped my cheek as he continued to thrust into me, hitting my throat harder than before. Tears dripped from the corners of my eyes, and he wiped one away with the pad of his thumb. "Lovely." He cupped his balls and massaged them while keeping one hand on my cheek. "Show me before you swallow."

"Yes, sir."

He moaned again as he pounded into my mouth, fucking me aggressively and stretching out my throat. His fingers moved to my neck, and he gripped me hard right before he burst. "Open your mouth."

I opened my mouth and stuck out my tongue.

He aimed his cock and squirted the mounds of white seed onto my tongue, giving me so much I could actually feel the weight. He stroked himself as he finished, his eyes heavy. "Fuck..." He stared at his handiwork while some of his come stuck to his fingers. "Swallow."

I retracted my tongue. "Yes, sir."

His eyes darkened all over again.

I swallowed, getting everything down into my belly. The warm water still pounded onto the tile floor, and I was still on my knees. I didn't notice the discomfort until the fun ended. Now my knees were sore, and my tits were flushed from massaging them. Even though I swallowed, I could still taste him on my tongue.

His thumb brushed along my bottom lip. "Now it's my turn to get on my knees."

When I woke up the next morning, Crewe was gone.

I still didn't know his schedule. Sometimes, he was there when I woke up, and sometimes, he wasn't. A breakfast tray was usually brought to my room, but eating alone wouldn't help my situation.

I looked through the closet until I found a tight pink sundress and a nice cardigan. It was a little fancy, but it hugged my curves in a way that made them noticeable. I did my hair and makeup, putting more effort into my appearance than ever before.

I walked downstairs and saw Dunbar in the massive entryway, exactly where his post usually was. I did my best to ignore him as I walked across the large room and toward the rest of the castle. Crewe was probably in the drawing room or in the courtyard.

"Where do you think you're going?"

I ignored Dunbar's cold voice and kept my head high.

"I asked you a question, bitch." He made his way toward me, his heavy footsteps amplified in the room.

Before he could grab me and start another war, I turned around but kept my distance. "I'm looking for Crewe. He's not worried about me running, so neither should you."

His bushy eyebrows connected in a single, straight line. He had a large nose that was the size of my fist, and he had a large mole near his chin. He wasn't pretty to look at, and he was definitely mean. "When it comes to cunts like you, I'm always worried."

If he touched me, I was gonna kick him in the balls as hard as I could. "I just want to speak to Crewe. As his woman, I have the right to do that."

"You aren't his woman," he said with a chuckle. "You're just one of his whores."

My temper snapped like a stretched rubber band. I clocked him right in the nose, giving him a powerful right hook that he had no idea was coming. I felt his nose break under my hit, and I got unbelievable satisfaction out of the damage. "Call me that again, and see what happens."

He staggered back as the blood dripped down his face. It took him a second to understand my hit was the source of the damage. Once everything came into place, he looked at me like he wanted to kill me.

Like, actually kill me.

He pulled out his gun.

Shit. "Crewe!" I ran as fast as I could even though I could never outrun a bullet. If Dunbar caught up to me, I was dead meat. "Crewe!" I had no idea where he was. I just hoped he was in the castle and he could hear me.

Dunbar charged me down and shoved me hard to the ground, making me slide across the tile. "Let's see how you look with a bloody nose, bitch!" He grabbed my neck and squeezed so hard I couldn't breathe. He raised the butt of his gun and prepared to slam it down onto my face.

Fuck, this was going to hurt.

"Get. Off. Her." Crewe's authoritative voice was enough to stall Dunbar's hand before it hit me. He stopped just inches away from my face, the metal of the gun nearly crushing my nose. The force would have set off a geyser of blood and permanently scarred my nose.

Dunbar stayed on top of me but dropped his weapons. "But she—"

"Get off of her." Crewe kicked him in the stomach so he would roll off me. He kneeled down and examined me even though I only had a few scratches on my arms from falling onto the stone. "Lovely, are you alright?" His powerful arms wrapped around me. He examined my face for any bruises.

"I'm fine." I looked at my arms and saw the burns from sliding across the floor.

Dunbar got to his feet and wiped the blood onto his sleeve. "She was trying to sneak away—"

Crewe held up his hand and dismissed him. "Disappear."

A grimace stretched across Dunbar's face, an explosive anger he could barely bottle inside. He wanted to get a word in but knew defying Crewe was a bad idea. He holstered his gun and finally walked away, his shoulders stiff with threat.

Crewe's hands pulled my hair off of my face as he examined me. "You're sure you're alright?"

I nodded. "I was walking by, and Dunbar said some stuff to me—"

"I'll handle him. Don't worry about him anymore."

I hoped that meant Crewe was going to fire him. Dunbar had had it out for me since the day I came around. This was the third time he'd hit me.

Crewe helped me to my feet before he cradled me against his chest. One hand moved into my hair while his other hand wrapped around my waist. He looked down at me like he was examining me again, making sure I was okay. "If Dunbar had left a scar on you, I would have killed him. I can't have a bloody date to the opening next weekend."

I was automatically offended by the statement. He didn't care about my safety, just about my presentation. Making him fall for me seemed even more unlikely now.

His thumb brushed along my cheek before he lifted my chin. "What happened?"

"I was walking by, and he called me a whore…so I punched him."

He sighed and shook his head. "No wonder why he came after you."

"Well, I don't appreciate being called a whore. Anytime I leave the room, he treats me like a criminal."

"What were you doing?"

"Looking for you."

"Did you tell him that?"

"Yes. I'm telling you, the guy just hates me."

Now that he knew I was okay, he looked down at my outfit. He seemed to like it because his mood picked up slightly. "You look pretty."

"Thanks…" The compliment seemed sincere, and that made me melt like butter.

"What did you want to see me for?"

I shrugged. "I missed you…" I held my breath after I said the words, unsure how he would receive them. I was jacking up the affection, and I was afraid he would recognize its lack of sincerity. I went from telling him off all the time to needing him. He wasn't stupid, so he might catch on.

But he didn't seem to find it suspicious. His eyes softened in reaction, and his thumb moved to the corner of my mouth. He stared at my lips before he leaned in and kissed me, a soft and gentle caress that made me feel like something more besides his prisoner. "Here I am. At your service."

"Can we have breakfast? Then go back to the room."

"I already ate." He looked down my dress to my cleavage line. "But I have some time…"

I climbed on the edge of the bed with my legs spread apart and my heels still on.

Crewe came up behind me, and he stilled when he realized I didn't have panties on. "Jesus Christ…" He undid his slacks and allowed his cock to come free, pulsing and thick. He positioned himself at my entrance then shoved himself inside me in one fluid motion.

I leaned forward slightly and closed my eyes, surprised how incredible he felt. "Crewe…"

"Lovely, I love it when you say my name." He gripped the back of my neck and shoved my face into the mattress, making my back curve at a deeper angle so my pussy was more accessible to him. He let his dick rest inside me for a second before he began to thrust.

I wanted him to enjoy me, to enjoy me on a scale he never enjoyed the others. I needed to seduce him with sex and affection, so I did something I'd never done before. I sucked my forefinger into my mouth then fingered my ass so he could see.

He slowed down to watch me, his pants turning into moans. "London…"

It was the first time he'd ever said my name during sex. He usually called me by my pet name, but never my true name. I fingered myself harder, pushing my forefinger in and out. I'd never done any ass play, so the action felt even more foreign. But I did what I had to do to survive. No one could judge me for that.

"Damn, you're incredible."

The more aroused he was, the wetter I became. I could feel his cock thickening inside me, reaching a new level of hardness. My drenched pussy provided the ideal lubrication so he could slide through with perfect friction. "I want your come…"

His fingers dug into my hips. "It's coming, Lovely. Keep fingering that asshole, and it'll be here."

I moaned through my actions, getting into it when I didn't expect to enjoy it. I didn't expect to enjoy anything with Crewe, but I realized he was the best sex I'd ever had. When I slept with other men, I never expected to have an orgasm. And when it did happen, I was grateful. But with Crewe, I came every time. It was a standard that guided my expectations. My life had been stripped from me, but at least I was getting the best sex of my life.

I moaned into the comforter as I came, squeezing his cock until it was bruised. I felt my pussy pool with more moisture from the climax. Now I was so wet I was dripping on the bed.

"Fuck…" He gave a few more pumps before he stilled inside me, his cock balls deep. He released inside me as he grabbed my wrist and squeezed. In the middle of his climax, he gave a few more pumps, shoving his come deeper inside me.

That made me moan again, knowing how much he wanted me to take his seed.

He wrapped his arm around my chest and pulled me up, making my back hit his collared shirt. He breathed into my ear canal, his cock slowly softening inside me. I pulled my finger out of my asshole and rested it on my thigh, my breathing still haywire. "I. Love. This. Pussy." He gently moved his cock inside me, pushing through the mounds of our come. "So. Fucking. Much."

6

CREWE

Dunbar walked into my office, his nose and eyes blue from where London had punched him. "You wanted to see me, sir?" He took a seat in the chair facing my desk.

"Get up." He didn't deserve to sit in that chair anymore. I was glad London punched him in the face. That woman could hold her own, and I respected her for it. In fact, it was a turn-on.

Dunbar tried to hide the irritated look on his face before he rose to his feet again.

"You're changing places with Dimitri. You'll be on the tower watch from now on." He would be required to stay outside during the night, sitting in one of the cars or walking the perimeter in the freezing cold.

Dunbar's eyes flashed with anger. "Sir, I can assure you—"

"You've been my right-hand man forever. That's the only reason why I'm not firing you altogether. You're lucky you get to keep your job at all."

He opened his mouth as if he wanted to argue again.

"London told me you have it out for her. At first, I didn't believe her, but now I've seen it with my own eyes. You are to have no interaction with her at all. Don't even speak to her."

"But sir, she's tried to escape before, and I—"

"She's not gonna run," I said coldly. "You know I have plenty of leverage over her. Unless she starts hating her brother, we're fine."

"But what if she figures out we implanted a fake?" he asked. "Then she'll be a loose cannon."

"How would she figure that out?" I snarled. "She's not a mind reader."

He took a deep breath as he tried to think of something that would persuade me. "Sir, I apologize, and I promise I'll be—"

"You blew your chance, Dunbar. Maybe when I cool off in a few months, I'll reinstate you. But for now, you're on tower duty. Get out of my office." I stared him down and dared him to defy me. One more word out of him and he would be risking his position entirely.

Dunbar must have known I was at the end of my patience because he gave a quick nod. "Yes, sir. Thank you, sir."

That's what I wanted to hear.

I had a hard time getting anything done that day because my mind kept wandering to the sexy brunette who shared my bed.

Watching her finger her asshole tested my performance. I wanted to come then and there, but only out of sheer stubbornness did I keep it together. Women only did that when they were asked to, and the fact that she did it on her own made me obsessive.

It was so hot.

Now I was distracted all the time, thinking about the woman who was constantly on my mind. With soft hair, softer skin, and moans that made my cock twitch, she was the most incredible thing in the world. She used to hate me with every fiber of her being, but that anger had slowly faded away.

She admitted that she needed me. That she trusted me. That she even liked me.

And I knew I liked her too.

My sexual appetite had been satiated the second I was inside her. Sasha called me when she was in town, but I told her I was too busy to see her. Miranda texted me when she was at the embassy, but I told her I was out of the country. I could have spent the night with them without doing anything.

But I didn't want to.

That was the most interesting part.

My prisoner gave me everything I needed. I satisfied my revenge at the same time and enjoyed the dynamics of our relationship. I was the boss, and she was the slave. It was pretty simple. I liked it that way.

I was glad I never gave her to Bones.

Eventually, I'd have to take a wife and have a family. Being a husband sounded like a bore, but fatherhood was something I actually looked forward to. I would need a woman who was happy in a loveless marriage. She could have her men on the side. I'd have my women, obviously. Perhaps we could be good friends who only loved our children.

So I didn't have to get rid of London entirely. But she certainly couldn't sleep in my bed every single night. She'd have to live off the property somewhere else so our relationship wouldn't arouse suspicion.

But London would never be able to have her own husband and family.

As crazy as that sounded, I actually felt a little sad.

That was strange.

Dimitri walked into my office, taking on his new role flawlessly. All of my men pined for my approval, wanting to be promoted. Dunbar had one of the highest positions in the crew, so he was one of the top billed. When I offered the position to Dimitri, he didn't hesitate before he accepted the role. Dunbar would probably turn sour against him, but he obviously didn't care. "Sir, the Duchess of Cambridge is here to see you."

You've got to be kidding me. "What?" It wasn't an intelligent thing to say, but I was shocked that she'd visited me twice.

"The Duchess of Cambridge." He repeated the title even though he knew I heard him the first time.

What the hell did this bitch want? I couldn't refuse an audience with royalty, but I'd told her not to come back here, and she obviously didn't believe my sincerity. If I entertained her, it would open the door to nonsense. "Tell her I'm unavailable. If she asks for my next opening, tell her I'm busy for the indefinite future." It was rude of me to behave that way, especially when her position was higher than mine, but if she only wanted to discuss her mistake of breaking off our engagement, I refused to listen to it.

"Yes, sir." Dimitri walked out again, leaving me alone in my office.

I'd just been thinking about London, that luscious ass and perfect tits, but now I was thinking about the betrayal that publicly humiliated me. I was combative and angry, my good day ruined about a past I couldn't erase.

I was on the phone with Ariel when London walked inside.

Dimitri must have allowed her to walk in because he assumed she had special access that others lacked. I would have told her to get out and inform Dimitri she was like everyone else, but when I saw her in a purple dress that hugged her tiny waist and her sexy legs in those nude pumps, I didn't want her to go anywhere. She'd curled her hair and pinned it up to the side, showing off her slender neck and cute face.

Ariel kept talking about our shipment, but I didn't listen.

Ever since we bought that gown in Italy, London had been going the extra mile to make herself look spectacular. Maybe the designer dress ignited an appreciation for outfits that she didn't have before. Now every time I saw her, I thought I was looking at a model. She used to wear jeans and t-shirts and didn't put a drop of makeup on her face, and she still looked stunning But now…there was no way to describe how phenomenal she looked.

Ariel continued on. "We have a large order near the Baltic Sea. They're asking for—"

"Let me call you back." I interrupted her without remorse, my eyes on the curvy woman walking right toward me.

"Sure." If Ariel knew why I was cutting her off, she would be pissed. But she probably assumed something more important had come up, so she hung up without complaint.

Without taking my eyes away from London's figure, I tossed the phone onto the desk. "You look nice." That was an understatement. She looked completely fuckable —even if she didn't finger herself.

"Thank you." She came around the desk, trailing her fingers along the ancient wood as she approached. Maybe she was doing it on purpose, but her sexiness seemed natural. She could walk into any room looking like that and turn heads everywhere. She stopped at my side, her short dress showing off her toned thighs. "Working hard?"

"I never work hard." My arms rested on the armrests, and I felt my cock harden in my slacks. My hand couldn't resist a touch of her smooth skin, so I wrapped my fingers around her thigh. I wanted to pull her onto my lap and sheathe myself inside her warm pussy.

Whenever I was in the same room as this woman, that was all I ever thought about. She infected my mind like a poison.

"I hope that's not true. Don't want to be homeless."

The corner of my mouth rose in a smile. "I'll always take care of you, Lovely." My fingers trailed to the back of her knee and to her calf. She had strong muscles for a small person, probably because she was on her feet all day when she was in school. My hand moved back up her thigh and underneath her dress until I gripped her left cheek.

Perky and soft.

"Is there something I can do for you?" My fingers felt the lace of her panties.

"I'm hungry."

"You know where the kitchen is." I had a chef working day and night when I was in town. When I was elsewhere, he got to take a vacation.

"I don't like eating alone all the time. It's boring."

"Are you asking if you can have lunch with me?"

Her eyes narrowed at the way I worded my sentence. "No. I'm not asking if I can have lunch with you. I'm telling you we should eat together."

The corner of my mouth rose in a smile, loving that feistiness. I would never want her to stop setting me straight. It was something I loved about her, even though I would never admit it. She wasn't docile, obedient, or quiet. That was how I liked her—most of the time. "When you put it like that…it's not like I'm doing anything anyway."

"I hope you do something productive while you're in here all day."

I shrugged. "That's debatable. Time passes, but I never feel like I'm getting anything done."

"Then you should fire Ariel."

London would love that. "She's not the problem. Without her, I wouldn't be productive at all."

"I'll believe it when I see it." She stepped away, so my hand dropped back to my side. "Come on, I'm hungry."

"You're bossy today." I stared at her ass as she walked to the door.

"I'm just hungry." She turned around with her hand on her hips. "Now feed your woman."

My woman? Instead of shooting her down, I actually liked the title. She was my slave, and I liked possessing her. "Wouldn't want you to get grouchy." I rose from the chair and buttoned the front of my suit. I walked up behind her, thinking about taking her on my desk when the meal was over. My arm slipped around her waist, and I walked into the hallway with her tucked into my side. "What are you in the mood for?"

"I'm not picky."

I was over a foot taller than her, but my arm was long enough to scoop around her waist. I liked her wide hips and slender stomach. She was petite but still womanly. We entered the large kitchen where my chef stood in front of the series of stoves.

"Hello, sir. What can I get for you?" He wore a tall chef's hat, and I wondered how he balanced it on his head all day.

I turned to London. "No preference?"

"Surprise us," she said.

Chef Bingly smiled. "I can do that."

"Want to eat in the courtyard?"

London lit up like that was the most exciting thing to happen to her all week. "Yes."

I guided her down the hallway again until we reached the courtyard that stood between two of the main fortifications. It had a great view of the countryside and the mountains in the far distance. The gardens were properly maintained, and they were blooming with roses of various colors. A fountain dripped continuously, providing the sound of falling water as the backdrop.

London felt a pink rose in her fingertips and smelled it before she examined the gardens further. She looked at the concrete statues and the bushes trimmed in the likenesses of safari animals.

I took a seat in one of the white chairs under the umbrella and watched. "I thought Ariel took you out here once before?"

"I didn't really get a chance to enjoy it." She grabbed a red rose from one of the bushes then tucked the stem behind her ear. The color contrasted against her fair skin but complimented the purple dress she wore. It was an accessory that fit perfectly. "She was insulting me the entire time."

"She tends to do that."

She took the seat across from me as one of the maids came out. She brought coffee and water, alone with a small vase of flowers. She nodded before she walked away, trying to be so quiet that we wouldn't notice her.

London added some cream to her coffee.

"I thought you liked it black." It was something I noticed the second she came into my possession. She had been too argumentative to speak to, so I'd had to study her to understand her.

"I already had a cup this morning. The acid hurts my stomach unless I soften it."

I nodded then poured my own mug.

"I'm surprised you still have a stomach with all that poison you drink."

I'd classify myself as an alcoholic. I just held my liquor well, so I didn't have any behavioral issues. London was the only one to mention my love for scotch. Everyone else didn't notice or didn't have the audacity to point it out. "Maybe I'm a cow."

She raised an eyebrow before she drank her coffee. "What?"

"Because they have four stomachs."

"Ooh…" She finally let out a chuckle. "I wasn't sure where you were going with that."

I liked watching her face light up with a smile. When I was the one who made her laugh, it was even better. When she coated her eyelashes in mascara, they were thick and dark and contrasted against her green eyes. In that moment, she was absolutely lovely. I wished I could take a picture of her. If I pulled out my camera, it would probably ruin the moment.

"So seriously, how many glasses of scotch do you drink a day?"

I shrugged. "I don't know. I've never counted."

"What would you estimate?"

I thought about the average day and how many glasses I had for lunch, while I sat in my office, and at dinnertime. Plus, all the scotch I drank before bed. "I don't know… six or seven glasses…sometimes nine or ten."

Her jaw nearly dropped, and her eyes popped open. "Nine or ten…?"

Was that a lot?

"That's insane. Your liver must be corroded."

I wouldn't know. I hadn't seen a doctor in years. "I feel fine." I still hit the gym hard every single day and ran my empire without a problem.

"That's just not good for you, Crewe. It's fine to drink… but not that much."

Instead of putting any value into what she said, I concentrated on the unspoken meaning of her words. "You sounds concerned."

"I am concerned. Alcohol at that level isn't healthy."

"I've been drinking like that for a long time. Don't worry about it."

"How can I not worry about it?" she demanded. "You're gonna drown yourself."

My love for scotch began when I was young. When I opened up my own distillery, it became worse. Getting lost in a smooth glass of amber liquid was the best way to chase away my depression. It was the best cure for nightmares.

"How do you even think when you're drunk all the time?"

"I think better, actually."

She rolled her eyes. "I'm not trying to sound bossy, but you really should cut it back. You'll need a liver transplant before you turn forty."

"And then I can keep going for another forty years."

Now she just glared at me.

"If I'm not mistaken, it sounds as if you care about me."

Her glare faded, but she still wore a serious look. "Because I do care about you, Crewe. But you already knew that."

My heart rate picked up slightly, and I felt arousal that wasn't caused by just her outfit. Hearing a confession like that inflated my ego bigger than it already was. She was being held here against her will, but she somehow felt a connection with me.

I was glad the feeling was mutual.

"I want you to cut back."

If anyone else had made that request of me, I wouldn't even consider it. But I loved the way her face darkened in concern. I loved knowing she cared about me, that she wanted me to live a long and healthy life. The longer I lived, the longer she was my prisoner. But that didn't seem to bother her.

"Crewe."

"How much are we talking?" I wanted to keep listening to this, to hear her beg me to take care of myself. She sounded like a nagging wife, but I actually liked it.

"Three to four glasses a day."

I laughed because it was absurd. "I have four glasses by the end of lunch."

"Well, you're gonna have to space it out. Drink more water."

"There's water in scotch."

That glare was back.

I smiled because I liked the look. "Five to six."

"Even that is too much. Three to four."

I shook my head. "There's no way I could do that. Just being honest."

"Baby steps. Cut back one drink a day until you reach four."

She made it sound so easy. "I'm addicted, Lovely. I need it."

"You can always replace it with something else."

"Cigars?"

Now that glare was more ferocious. "No smoking."

"Then what?"

"Sex always works."

I raised an eyebrow, hoping that was some kind of offer. "Sex, huh?"

"Yeah. When you get the urge, come looking for me instead."

Scotch for sex. That didn't sound so bad. "You'll get my mind off it?"

"I'll certainly try."

With an offer like that, cutting back actually sounded possible. "I'll try."

"There's no try. You seem like a man who always succeeds. Make this a success."

"You should be a motivational speaker, you know that?"

She shook her head. "Very little things motivate me, besides health. I want everyone to live a long and happy life, free from disease that's self-induced. I hate seeing it. It's the worst."

I always forgot about her medical background. When I looked at her, I just saw a beautiful woman at my beck and call. I didn't think about her passions or her previous life. None of that seemed to matter. "Looks like I have a private physician."

"I don't know about that...never got my license." The accusation was heavy in her voice.

I let it wash over me without any effect. If she didn't want to be there, she wouldn't be so seductive, so flirtatious. I suspected she wanted to stay there with me, to live like royalty every single day without having to lift a finger. Every woman wanted to be pampered. She was no different.

I held her hand as we walked back to my office. We had a nice lunch and talked about the beautiful weather. As if we were a couple, we were comfortable in mutual silence. We didn't always need to talk, but when we did, it was nice.

But I didn't feel like being nice right now.

I stopped in front of my office door. "I have a phone call to make. When I'm done, I'm going to go upstairs and see you naked on the bed, flat on your stomach. Do you understand?" If she wanted me to quit drinking like an alcoholic, she'd definitely have to distract me.

These situations were the only ones where she obeyed. Any other time, I had a face full of attitude. "Yes, sir."

"Good." I grabbed her wrist then pressed a kiss to the corner of her mouth. I had a lot of dirty things in mind for her. It would be a shame not to put that beautiful ass to good use. "See you in a few." I turned my back on her and walked into my office. I didn't have any such phone call to make. I just wanted to give her time to prepare for me. I intended to do something new with her, something she'd probably never experienced.

Hopefully, she would like it.

I sat at my desk and eyed the bottle of scotch sitting next to my laptop. I didn't know how many glasses I'd had that day, but I was certain I was already over the limit. Cutting down would be a lot more difficult than I'd anticipated. It'd only been five minutes, and I was already struggling.

I really did have a drinking problem.

My cell phone rang, and I pulled it out of my pocket and glanced at the screen, expecting to see Ariel getting back to me with news about the shipment. I was supposed to call her back and never did. But she knew I was forgetful and busy.

But it was Josephine.

Why the fuck wouldn't this bitch just disappear?

I didn't need any more rumors about my love life. She humiliated me once, and I wouldn't be dragged into scandal again. If people assumed I was contemplating taking her back, that would be even worse than when she left me to begin with.

That made me look like the biggest pussy in the world.

I didn't believe in forgiveness.

Just ruthlessness.

I swiped my thumb across the screen and answered. I pressed the phone to my ear but didn't say anything, too annoyed to actually form words with my mouth. I'd made it abundantly clear she didn't have any chance with me, but apparently, that didn't mean shit to her. "If you're interested in ordering Highland Scotch for a party, you can always call Ariel. If you're inviting me to a social event, invitations by mail are welcome. Any other inquiries are inappropriate, and frankly, annoying." I was never this cold to her when we were together, not even when she pissed me off, but when she decided to be with someone else, I shut the door on her forever. It wasn't about getting my heart broken. It was about the disloyalty.

I hated disloyalty.

She made a promise to me—and she fucking broke it.

Josephine breathed into the phone, obviously offended by my introduction. She didn't have a backbone the way Ariel did. She was fragile. A few insults were enough to cripple her into sobs.

"Crewe, I just want to talk to you."

"About what?" I asked coldly. "We aren't friends, so I don't see what there is to talk about."

"I'm sorry to bother you…I really am."

"No, you aren't," I snapped. "If so, you wouldn't have dropped by yesterday. And you wouldn't be calling me now."

"It's just…my father is in the hospital."

I hadn't heard the news. Maybe they were keeping it quiet. For just an instant, I felt sympathy. "I'm sorry to hear that, Josephine. Will he be alright?"

"He had a heart attack…" She cried into the phone. "The doctors say they think he'll be okay, but he's being observed overnight for a few more days. There's a blockage in one of his carotid arteries. They need to operate."

I didn't remember my father very much. All I had were pictures of him. The only memories I had were ones I made up. When I saw a picture of us playing catch outside on the lawn, I pretended we were both baseball fans even though we never followed the international sport. "I'm sure he'll be okay." I had no idea if her father would be okay, but I wanted to say what she wanted to hear.

"I don't know…I just came home to get some sleep. I'd been there for a few days."

Except when she came to my home.

"I was hoping you could stop by…or I could go over there."

The question made me angry, but I swallowed my rage out of respect for her situation. "Where's Andrew?"

"He's in Africa with UNICEF. He'll be gone for another week. He said he couldn't leave right now…"

Nothing would have stopped me from being by her side if we were still together. But that ship had sailed. "I can't join you, Josephine. You know that."

"Please…I don't know what to do. I'm so scared, and I don't want to be alone right now."

No way in hell was I going over there. If someone saw me, it would look really bad. Not that I wanted to go over there anyway. "Josephine, I'm not your fiancé anymore. And I'm not your friend either. Let's not forget how we got here. You left me for Andrew. You have to stand by your choice now."

"I said I made a mistake. How many times do I have to repeat it?"

"You couldn't repeat it enough times," I said coldly. "But it wouldn't change anything anyway."

She cried quietly into the phone, trying to cover up the sound of her tears. "I know you still love me…"

"I really don't." Any love I had for her disappeared the day she betrayed me. I stopped respecting her. I stopped caring about her. It made me realize that everything meaningful we had never meant anything at all. Within the snap of a finger, I was over it.

And I never looked back.

"I don't believe you," she whispered.

"I don't care," I said coldly. "I'm sorry about your father. I truly am. I hope he has a speedy recovery and he's back on his feet soon."

"Crewe—"

"Please don't call me again, Josephine." I hung up before she could get another word in. Her problems weren't my problems anymore. I wasn't being stubborn, just authoritative. You couldn't humiliate me in front of the whole world and come back to me when you needed something. I respected myself too much for that.

It took me a few seconds to remember what was waiting for me upstairs. I eyed the scotch and felt my restraint slip away. I snatched the bottle and poured another glass, forgetting what London asked me to do. I downed the amber liquid and felt the burn all the way down my throat.

But it didn't burn as much as my anger.

7

LONDON

I lay on the bed like he instructed, naked and flat on my belly. Taking orders from him was easy when it came to stuff like this. I wasn't offended at being bossed around, not when he had that smoldering look in his eyes. Obeying was my best course of action—and the best way to get into his heart.

The best way for me to escape.

He walked into the room minutes later and shut the door behind him. His actions were loud, his heavy shoes hitting the floor heavily just before he dropped his jacket to the ground. He was announcing his presence as loudly as possible as he approached the bed.

My wrists were yanked behind my back, and he secured his tie around my wrists. He tugged harder than necessary, forcing my shoulders back off the bed. He tied the silky fabric into a strong knot before he undressed himself. His shirt hit the floor, following by everything else.

I tried to keep my breathing calm, but it continued to accelerate. It was a combination of my discomfort and my arousal. I could sense how much he wanted me based on his quick movements. He was anxious, even a little angry.

When he was finally naked, he opened one of his drawers and pulled out a bottle of lube.

He never needed that with me. I was always soaked for him. He'd commented on it countless times.

"What's that for?"

Crewe never answered. He grabbed a bottle and popped the lid off. Then he poured the liquid directly on top of my ass.

My body prickled at the cold liquid, and I looked over my shoulder to see the amber color. Of course, it was scotch.

It soaked into the blanket and the sheets underneath, but he didn't care.

His hands moved to either side of my body, and he leaned down to kiss me. His lips started on my left cheek then moved to the right. The kisses started off gentle and quickly accelerated into something much more aggressive. His tongue lapped at my skin as he moved to the center of my cheeks. Then he pressed his face deeper into the crack and swiped his tongue across my asshole.

I tensed when he felt him, never having experienced that before. He licked the scotch directly off my opening, tasting me as well as the alcohol. My wrists automatically tested the soft fabric of his tie, my back arching and my lips parting.

His tongue greeted my opening slowly, licking the entrance as if he were asking for permission to come inside. His kisses and caresses turned more aggressive, and he shoved his tongue inside me and tasted me in a way no man ever had.

My head rested on the bed, and I took a deep breath as my nerve endings fired off in alarm. I'd never been touched that way, never been kissed at my back entrance like that. If he'd told me he was going to do this before he did it, I would have said I wasn't into it. But the longer I felt him, the less intrusive it seemed. His hand gripped my right cheek and pulled it to the side, giving him more access to my asshole. He kissed me harder with more force, lubricating my entrance with just his saliva.

I wasn't sure if I enjoyed it or not. It was just so weird to be kissed in an area I never let anyone get close to. None of the other men in my life even tried to visit the location, but Crewe poured scotch all over it and lapped it up like he'd been in the desert all week.

His breathing increased, and I felt his hard dick press against me when he moved sometimes. He blew warm air across my skin before he kissed me again, his tongue diving deeper and deeper.

A quiet moan escaped my mouth when I felt him take me more aggressively. If I were going to get him to see me as more than a slave, I'd have to do all the things he enjoyed —even if they were strange. So far, enjoying things had never been a problem. But this was too weird, too unusual.

He dove his tongue into my entrance once more before he pulled his mouth away and stood up. He grabbed the bottle of lube, popped the cap, and then squirted it onto my ass.

Now I figured out what the lube was for.

When he fucked my pussy, he stretched me to the breaking point. It always felt good, but it was also a little painful. I never minded the pain because everything else was so good. But taking him in my rear was not something I found appetizing.

He squirted the lube onto his length and massaged it into the skin, coating his cock with the shiny liquid.

I looked at him over my shoulder. "I'm not into this."

His dark eyes turned to me, and they continued to throb with desire as though I hadn't said anything at all. "You've done it before?"

"No, I—"

"Then you're going to try." He crawled on top of the bed and positioned himself over me. His cock rubbed against my slippery cheeks, and he dug in his hips as he ground against me.

"That's an exit, not an entrance."

He craned his neck over my shoulder and looked down at me. "Every hole in your body is an entrance for me." He directed his length to my asshole and slowly began to push.

I yanked on the tie, assuming I could snap it in half since the material was soft, but it didn't go anywhere. It was snugly secured in place. I tried again, but it seemed like it tightened the knot even more.

He pressed his head into my entrance, and the second he was inside me, I felt the stretching. My body was being pulled apart in ways it never had been before. I felt the pain at his intrusion, my body automatically wanting to push him out.

His mouth moved to my ear. "Relax."

"I have a dick going into my ass. How am I supposed to relax?"

He chuckled, his warm breath falling over my canal. "It'll feel good. When have I ever made you feel anything but good?" He kissed the shell of my ear then sealed his mouth over mine. He kissed me slowly, his lips moving with mine. As he distracted me, he slowly inserted his cock farther, stretching my asshole in a way it'd never been stretched before. I was pinned to the bed with my wrists bound, forced to take his impressive cock.

He ended our kiss and looked into my eyes instead, watching my reaction.

He moved farther and farther, making my breath quicken and my body tense. It was the most unusual sensation I'd ever felt. He wasn't even completely inside me yet, and I felt full. I didn't think I could take any more of him. "Crewe…"

"Stay with me." He pushed farther until his length was completed inserted, all nine inches pulsing. He wasn't just long, but thick. The pressure was intense, and I tugged on the tie again.

"It hurts…" I never admitted weakness to him out of principle, but having him completely inside me like this was a brand-new feeling. It was a lot more intimate than being slapped across the face or grabbed by the neck.

"I know." He moved his lips to my temple. "It always hurts the first time." He started to rock his hips slowly, inserting his length and gently pulling it out. No matter how subtle his moves were, the sensation was intense. He breathed into my ear canal, his desire heavy in his breath.

A quiet grunt escaped his throat as he stretched my asshole over and over.

I kept my shoulders back and tried to remain relaxed. The tenser I became, the more it hurt. My eyes smarted from the firing of my nerve endings, and a few drops pooled at the corners of my eyes and dripped down my cheeks.

Crewe inserted his full length inside me then grabbed my chin. He tilted my face toward him so he could get a good view of my expression. He moaned at the sight of my tears then started to move again, giving me his length over and over. "Fuck, you're pretty when you cry."

My body shook as his thrusts increased. He started off slow, but now he couldn't restrain his excitement. He rocked into me harder, making the bed shake as our body weight shifted forward over and over. "Such a tight asshole."

Listening to his excitement made me forget the discomfort I was feeling. My body finally loosened, and the tears stopped pooling in my eyes. His length started to feel good inside me, just as it did when he was deep in my pussy. My clit rubbed against the comforter on the bed the harder he shook me, and that extra stimulation brought me to a heavenly level of pleasure.

Crewe picked up on my enjoyment. "I always make you feel good, Lovely." He thrust into me harder, giving me his length at a greater speed than before. He was no longer gentle, taking me like we'd done this countless times.

The more vigorous his movements, the more it hurt. But it also felt better at the same time, feeling his length more intensely and dragging my clit across the sheets. My wrists instinctively pulled on the tie again as I began to writhe, moans automatically pouring out of my mouth.

His pants increased the harder he moved inside me. "You like my cock in your mouth and your pussy. Now you like it in your ass."

The heat seared my body and burned me from the inside out.

"Tell me."

I shook with his thrusts. "I like your cock in my ass."

He fucked me harder, giving it to me ruthlessly. "I want more than that."

I felt the heated warning in my belly as the orgasm approached. I knew I was going to climax. I could feel it in my bones. "I love your cock in my ass…"

He thrusts turned into pounds, and he fucked my ass ruthlessly.

I was gonna come. I could feel it deep inside me. It slowly circled through my nerves before it migrated down into my gut. With a fiery explosion, it ignited. My face pressed against the mattress, and my back arched as I writhed. I let out a scream for the entire castle to hear, but I didn't care if they overheard my pleasure. Crewe fucked me harder to egg me on, and I was carried into a powerful oblivion that lasted for minutes. My wrists yanked on the tie until the material dug into my wrists, burning me from the powerful friction.

"Lovely…" After a few more heated pumps, he came with a moan. "Fuck." His cock pulsed inside me as he released, filling me with mounds of arousal. His breathing was loud next to my ear, and he stayed put until every single drop was deep inside me.

He pressed his forehead against the back of my head, his chest warm and covered with sweat. He breathed with me, coming down from his high as I did the same. His pulse was strong against my back, his body fatigued after the way he took me roughly. With a sigh, he climbed off of me and slowly pulled his cock out.

My ass immediately tightened when he was gone, and it felt strange without him deep inside me.

He left the bed and walked into the shower without saying another word to me. I never realized I expected his affection until he didn't give it. He usually kissed me or caressed my hair with his fingertips when we were finished. But now, I felt like a meaningless whore who was just there for a quick fuck.

He'd never made me feel like that before.

I left the bed and cleaned up before I stripped the sheets. Maybe he didn't care about the scotch getting into the mattress, but I certainly did. I placed them in the hallway and knew the maids would take care of it.

Sometimes I thought I was making progress with Crewe, making him look at me differently than he used to. I thought he was kinder, gentler. He went out of his way to look out for me, hold my hand when I was scared on the plane and defend me when Dunbar lost his temper. But now, it was just like the first day I arrived.

He didn't give a damn about me.

What happened? We had lunch together, and everything seemed fine. Then he came upstairs in a brooding mood.

I'd ask, but he would never tell me.

I couldn't get discouraged and give up. I had to keep going if I ever wanted to get out of here. Being insignificant would just keep me here longer. If he ever got bored with me, he might sell me or kill me.

I couldn't let that happen.

I walked into the bathroom and saw him standing underneath the water. He'd just shampooed his hair, so he closed his eyes and tilted his head so he could rinse the suds away. If you took away the constant hostility, the fact that he was kidnapped me, and the sudden changes in his mood, he was a perfect man. With a body carved out of marble and a face more handsome than any model on any billboard I'd ever seen, he was beautiful. Sexy and strong, he had a rugged jawline and corded veins across his hands and forearms. If we'd met in another life, I suspect I'd be obsessed with him.

But that wasn't reality.

He was my enemy, the man holding my brother's life hostage as well as my own. Despite my attraction, I would never forget what my objective was. Sometimes his kiss softened my resolve. Sometimes I felt safe when he protected me. Sometimes I was grateful he was sleeping beside me at night.

But that didn't change anything.

I stepped into the shower behind him and closed the door. The walls were made of glass, and the space was big enough to fit four people. He must have heard the door but didn't give any indication that he knew I was behind him.

My hands reached his lower back, and I slowly slid up the grooves of muscle until I reached his shoulder blades. My fingertips pressed lightly into the skin, giving him affection without digging my claws into him.

He stayed under the shower and didn't move, as if I weren't there at all.

I pressed a kiss between his shoulder blades, tasting the drops of water that fell from his hair.

He turned his head slightly, at last giving me a reaction.

My arms circled his waist, and I rested my head against his back, standing under the water with him. I felt his strong heartbeat against my palm, noticing it was still beating hard even though he'd been in the shower for several minutes.

He finally turned around, giving me the attention I silently commanded. His powerful arms circled my body and rested in the steep curve of my back. With wet hair and drops of water all over his body, he looked even sexier than he did when he was sweaty just moments ago. "You doing okay?"

Maybe my presence snapped him out of his bad mood. He seemed to be somewhere else as soon as we were finished, something weighing heavily on his mind. "Yeah…it hurt at first, but it got better as we went along."

He gripped my cheeks and massaged them. "It always hurts the first time. But it gets better with practice."

"I hope so."

"That was your first time, I take it?"

Was that not obvious enough? "Yes."

His eyes smoldered in delight. "Good."

"Good?" I asked, my attitude coming out.

"I wanted to be your first something."

"Well, you're the first man to kidnap me," I teased. "That's gotta count for something."

He chuckled. "Yeah, I suppose it does." He dropped his hands from my waist then grabbed a bar of soap. He wiped himself down and washed his dick. He was semihard, probably because he just squeezed my ass with his palms.

I squirted the shampoo into my hands and massaged it into my scalp. "Did you have a bad phone call?"

He stilled at the question, the bar of soap pressed to his chest. It took him a second to recover before he continued scrubbing himself. "Why do you ask?"

"As soon as you walked into the room, you were in a different mood."

"I wanted to fuck you in the ass before lunchtime."

"That's not what I meant. As soon as we were finished, you were different. Like something is on your mind…" I knew better than to outright ask him what I wanted to know. He didn't share his secrets with me, and if I pushed him, he would only push back harder. If I ever wanted something from him, I had to manipulate him.

He looked down at me with a stern expression, clearly having no intention of answering me.

I shouldn't be surprised. I tilted my head under the water and rinsed the shampoo out of my hair. I'd already showered that day and I didn't need to wash my hair again, but I needed an excuse to stay under the water. I wanted this conversation to keep going, to continue bringing us closer together. "It's fine if you don't want to talk about it. But just remember, I'm your closest confidant in the world. There's no one I can share your secrets with. I'm always here for you if you need someone."

"Why would you be there for me when I haven't been there for you?" He stepped closer to me until his head was under the water again.

If I were too nice to him, he would know I was full of shit. Crewe wasn't stupid. In fact, he was calculating, cruel, and a genius. Everything he touched turned to gold. He had wealth, power, and supernatural intelligence. A man like that wouldn't have his position unless he was doing something right.

"You have been there for me."

"In what way?" he asked. "You just pointed out that I kidnapped you, drugged you and stole you from your warm bed." His mocha colored eyes had a darker appearance now that his mood had been tested.

"You didn't sell me to Bones." It was the most compassionate decision he ever made, to go back on his word to spare me the unbearable pain of slavery. He called me his slave now, but I didn't honestly feel like one. I always had the power to say no, something I truly valued. I always had a voice, an opinion. I got to eat when I was hungry. I got to sleep when I was tired. I knew Vanessa had it much differently than I did.

"That was for my own selfish reasons." His voice was colder than a winter morning.

"That's what you say, but I don't believe you." I think pity found its way into his heart and changed his mind. But he would never admit it, needing to keep up this cruel façade. "I'm scared of flying, and you always comfort me. When I have a nightmare, you help me get through it. When Dunbar hurt me, you protected me. You have to stick to your word by keeping me, but you certainly don't want to cause me pain. I think you're capable of being a good man, but you're doing everything in your power to prevent that from happening."

The water streamed down his face, and he didn't blink as he stared at me. Like a stone wall, he was impossible to decipher. He kept his thoughts hidden from me, adopting his stance of royalty and his countenance of mystery.

He set the bar of soap on the shelf then walked away. He silently dismissed the conversation, ending it right when we were in the middle of it. His usual flirtatious attitude disappeared the second lunch was over, and now the dark and tormented man remained behind. He grabbed a towel on his way and quickly wrapped it around his waist as he walked out, his large feet leaving a trail of footprints across the tile.

My objective was to get him closer to me, but I was certain I only pushed him further away. Sometimes it seemed like we were moving in a positive direction, but then we hit a wall and had to take steps backward. Perhaps Crewe had a heart that was incapable of love.

Or maybe he didn't have a heart at all.

He was gone for the rest of the evening, long after I finished dinner and got ready for bed. He usually returned to the bedroom after work or after dinner, but he was nowhere in sight. It was nearly midnight, which was the latest he'd ever been out.

I hoped he wasn't with someone else.

If he ran off to another woman, everything I'd done was for nothing. He was supposed to come to me for comfort, not one of his whores. When a painful throb started in my chest, I did my best to ignore it. I wasn't jealous. I simply felt defeated that I was nowhere closer to getting out of here.

That I would probably die here.

After midnight, he finally walked inside. I was in bed, so I continued to lie there in the dark, unsure if I wanted him to know I was awake.

He dropped his jacket on the ground, kicked his shoes off, and then stripped off everything else until there were small piles all over the hardwood floor. He usually took the time to place his laundry in the hamper or hang it up for the maids to be dry cleaned.

But he obviously didn't give a damn tonight.

I always wondered where he kept that transmitter that was linked to my brother's skull. I never saw it on him or noticed the outline in his pocket. He might keep it hidden away somewhere so I couldn't intercept it.

So he obviously didn't trust me.

He would be stupid to do so.

He washed his face and brushed his teeth in the bathroom before he came to bed and slid under the clean sheets. He always slept in the nude, so I assumed that was no different now. He stuck to his side of the massive king bed. We never cuddled while we slept. The only time he'd ever held me was when I had that nightmare a few weeks ago. While he held me and kissed me, that affection was purely sexual. He never offered me anything more tender, except the occasional kiss on the temple that was so rare I couldn't even recall the last time he did it.

I didn't want this distance between us. It reminded me of a husband and wife in a loveless marriage that was falling apart. He was out with other women while I slept alone. The only way to fill this void was to crawl on top of him and ride his dick.

I was nearly repulsed by the idea.

If he had been with someone else, he'd just kissed her. His hands had roamed over her naked body as he explored her curves. His cock had just been inside her, hopefully sheathed in a condom, but even if it was, it disgusted me.

I didn't want to be his sloppy seconds.

But I had no other choice. He had to see me as the woman he adored, the woman he couldn't get enough of. Most days, I did feel that way. But right now, I felt like a stranger. I felt like I wasn't even in that bed with him.

I swallowed my pride and tried not to think about what he was doing tonight. I tried not to picture the woman he was with, a woman far more beautiful than I was. I focused on my little apartment in New York City. It was a hole in the wall with busted appliances and noisy neighbors, but it was home.

This wasn't home.

I slid over the sheets as I approached his powerful body on the other side of the bed. He was lying on his back with his hand behind his head. His toned triceps led to his powerful chest and beautiful physique.

My hand slid over his chest, and I leaned down and pressed a kiss to his neck. My leg moved between his as I pressed myself against him, wearing his t-shirt and just my panties. I'd never seduced a man because I wasn't sexy enough to pull it off. But I did my best now, hoping he would take the bait.

He didn't. "What do you want?" He didn't push me off him, but he didn't respond to my affection either. He just lay there.

My first instinct was to slap him for being so harsh. But that wouldn't get me anywhere. "You must be really dull if you can't figure it out." I pulled the sheets down and straddled his hips.

He looked up at me, his gaze unreadable. His thoughts weren't always clear, but I could usually pick up on his mood. Right now, he was a blank canvas. He didn't seem angry or happy, just indifferent. "I'm not in the mood."

I was losing the battle, but I couldn't accept the defeat. "Well, I am…" I pulled my shirt over my head and tossed it on the floor. Thankfully, it was a little cold so my nipples automatically hardened, and my tits were firmer than usual.

Crewe's eyes immediately went to my chest, but he didn't move.

I crawled up his chest then kissed the line between his pecs and his chiseled stomach. My ass was in the air, and I suspected he was probably staring at it. I moved my kisses to his chin and then finally on his mouth.

He kissed me back, but it lacked any passion.

He must have been with someone else tonight. He'd never turned me down before. Normally, he wanted me around the clock, nonstop.

A burning pain thudded in my chest. I told myself I didn't care about the other woman, that I was just discouraged I wasn't making any progress. But the pain wouldn't stop. When I pulled away, I quickly hid my pain and got off him. "Fine. I want to wait for you, but I can do it on my own." I returned to my spot on the bed and did something I'd never done before.

I spread my legs and slid my fingers into my panties.

I touched my clit in a circular motion, doing my best to look as sexy as possible. For all I knew, I looked ridiculous. But I had to hope that this would work, that

Crewe would be enticed to come out of his brooding mood.

At first, I did it just for show. But the longer I touched myself, the more I liked it. I stopped caring about Crewe being in the room. I closed my eyes and felt my breathing grow deep and shallow. Erotic images came into my mind, Crewe on top of me as he thrust into me. He was the first thing I thought about once I became turned on, and I suspected that was because I'd been sleeping with him for months.

Nothing more meaningful than that.

My original plan was no longer in my mind, and now I just enjoyed the feel of my fingers. I writhed on the bed and closed my eyes, my back arching and my nipples hardening as they pointed to the ceiling. I couldn't catch my breath, and I felt the heat sear my body.

"Jesus fucking Christ…" Crewe finally left his side of the bed and crawled on top of me. His hips separated my thighs, and he pointed his rock-hard dick at my entrance. His thick head pushed forward before sliding completely inside me.

My hands gripped the back of his shoulders, and I moaned when I felt him between my legs. "Crewe…"

He pressed his mouth to mine and gave me a hard kiss, full of tongue and the kind of passion I wanted from him. His hand dug into my hair, and he fisted it aggressively, claiming me as his. "That was the hottest goddamn thing I've ever seen."

I spoke between kisses. "I prefer you to my fingers any day."

He moaned against my mouth. "Lovely…"

"I've been waiting for you to come home all evening… I need you."

He breathed against my mouth, his cock pulsing deep inside me.

My hands moved down his powerful chest as I felt his lips with mine. My hips rocked slightly, feeling him stretch my soaked pussy. "Fuck me slowly." My hands moved up his shoulders to the back of his head. His strands slid through the openings in my fingers. "Kiss me. Make me come."

He pulled his mouth away with an intense expression on his face. His eyes were darker than usual, and his jaw was tense as if he was angry. His entire body was tight with excitement. I could feel his cock thicken even more inside me. "Yes, Lovely." He started to move inside me, sliding in and out of my slickness. He took me slowly like I asked, and I was surprised he gave me what I wanted. I expected him to argue with me or just fuck me senseless. But he was in the moment with me—exactly what I wanted.

He hooked his arms behind my knees and pinned me underneath him, contorting my body until I was pressed hard against the mattress with his powerful body keeping me in place. He rocked his hips and clenched his ass every time he moved inside me, nine inches of his impressive cock hitting me every time.

His arms flexed, the intricate lines separating the different sections distinct and beautiful. His stomach was tight as he used his entire core to stabilize himself. It was much easier to fuck hard rather than slow, but his graceful physicality made it easy.

His mouth moved to mine, and he kissed me slowly, just the way I liked. Our mouths moved together, and his tongue would greet mine in the perfect intervals. Our tongues would slide past one another before he sucked my bottom lip into his mouth. No matter how criminal he was, he was still the best kisser I'd ever had. He made gentleness feel aggressive. He made slow feel fast. He made sex feel like a spiritual adventure of pleasure and ecstasy. I'd never been with a man who made me moan and writhe the way Crewe did.

"I'm gonna come…" My fingers dug into his hair, and I breathed into his mouth, feeling every inch of that cock hit me in the right spot. I was never vocal during sex, but I wanted Crewe to know how he made me feel, that he was the kind of man who made me feel like a woman.

He moaned quietly against my mouth. "I can feel it…"

My hands dragged down his shoulders, and I breathed against his mouth, too focused on the impending orgasm to even kiss him. My lips brushed against his, sometimes sticking together from their wetness.

I gripped his ass when I felt the explosive sensation hit me. Like a fire that burned every inch of my skin, I was molten hot. I pulled him against me harder, no longer wanting it to be slow and gentle. I wanted every inch over and over as I had an incredible orgasm that only he could ignite. I felt my come drench around his cock as he continued to move inside me, my arousal sheathing him like a glove.

My head rolled back, and I looked into his eyes, seeing the same desire on his face that was written all over mine.

I wasn't even aroused before he walked into the room, and now I felt satisfied, like I'd been wanting him all day. "Thank you…"

He kissed the corner of my mouth as he kept moving inside me. "My pleasure." His thrusts became harder, hitting me into the mattress as his balls spanked against my ass. He was preparing for a climax, to fill my pussy with all of his seed.

"No." I gripped his biceps as I felt him slide into me. "Make me come again." I kissed him hard, my tongue dancing around his as my nails dug into his skin. My pussy was so wet I wasn't sure if he could even feel the friction anymore.

He moaned into my mouth like that just turned him on even more. "I'd love to." He leaned farther over me so his pelvic bone could rub into my clit. He dug into me hard, igniting my throbbing nub in the heat of passion. His cock stretched me to maximum capacity, and the constant friction against my body made me pant with pleasure. It took far less time to bring me to a second climax than I expected.

"I'm already there…"

He slowed down his thrusts, controlling himself so he wouldn't blow his load quicker than I blew mine.

"God, Crewe…"

He gripped my hair and gave a slight tug, getting as much of me as he could.

I was stood on the threshold of an incredible orgasm, a blinding pleasure that would ignite me just like it did minutes ago. I was out of my mind with satisfaction, the hormones and the sweat destroying all inhibitions. "I love your cock…" I wanted to be everything he wanted, everything he fantasized about. They said the best way to a man's heart was through his stomach. But Crewe had a strict diet, so that would never work. The best way to his heart was through amazing sex.

"I love your pussy."

I hit my threshold when I saw the heated look in his eyes. I saw the way he looked at me, like I was the sexiest thing in the world. He made me feel beautiful with his restrained desire. He enjoyed making me come, not just getting off himself. He wanted to pump his seed inside me as much as I wanted to take it.

My second orgasm was as good as the first one. The heat burned my skin and made me writhe in a pool of my own sweat, but it felt so good. "Crewe, give me your come…" I clung to him desperately, moaning through the pleasure that lit me on fire.

He pushed me hard into the mattress as he pumped inside me, breathing hard as he gave me another incredible orgasm. He released a loud moan when he found his own release, filling me with mounds of his own come. "Fuck…"

I grabbed his hips and pulled him farther into me, loving all the seed he gave me. "Your come feels so good…"

His eyes focused on mine without blinking, steady and intense. "It feels even better giving it to you." Instead of pulling out right away, he blanketed my body with his and kissed me with the same passion as before. His cock slowly softened inside me, but he kissed me like he wanted to fuck me all over again.

I was fully satisfied, having two powerful orgasms right in a row with a gorgeous, sweaty man on top of me. But I didn't want it to end. I wanted to kiss him as much as he wanted to kiss me.

He pulled away then rubbed his nose against mine, his hair messy from the way I twirled it in my fingertips. He slowly pulled his soft cock out of me, leaving his load of come behind. He leaned back and examined me, seeing the heavy seed slowly seep out of me because so much was packed inside. "Damn…"

I was still high, so I wiped my fingers across my opening, getting his sticky come on my fingertips. I felt it drip down my fingers before I brought my hand to my mouth and sucked everything away.

Crewe watched every movement I made, his eyes wide with both shock and profound desire.

I licked more away before I circled my mouth with my tongue. "Yum."

Crewe watched me for several seconds, holding his powerful body on his arms. His cock started to harden all over again, so he moved back on top of me and pointed his head inside me. He hardened at a remarkable speed then pushed through his come and entered me once more. "I'm gonna fuck you all night."

"Thank you, sir."

He took a sharp breath like he'd been stabbed. The title floored him, cranking up his desire to an entirely new level. His cock was just as thick as the first round, and his desire seemed to be even greater.

When he fucked me again, he fucked me hard. He threw my legs over his shoulders and pinned me down like a man conquering an entire army. He possessed me with every thrust, destroyed me with every push. Our come moved together and got all over the sheets, but neither one of us cared.

And of course, he made me come again.

8

CREWE

Dimitri placed my second mug of coffee on the desk and silently dismissed himself.

I usually drank a cup in the morning, but today, I probably needed at least three cups. I didn't get any sleep last night, so I was exhausted.

Not that I was complaining.

I couldn't focus on any of my tasks because I kept thinking about that unbelievable woman upstairs in my bedroom. She was probably still asleep because she didn't have any reason to get up early. But by lunchtime, she'd better be ready for me.

206 | PENELOPE SKY

I was gonna fuck her even harder than I did last night.

I was in a pissed mood last night after Josephine called, begging me to show her compassion when she didn't deserve it. It stirred up feelings of rage that I couldn't control. I went out into town and drank at a bar alone, but that didn't make me feel any better.

Just made me feel worse.

The last thing I wanted was to screw my slave, but once she started touching herself, I was out of my mind. I couldn't get my cock inside her fast enough. And when he was there, he never wanted to leave.

He wanted to stay buried inside her forever.

I wiped the sleep from the corner of my eye for the third time and took a drink of my second coffee. I hadn't had any scotch today because I was too tired for that. At this rate, I really could quit cold turkey.

The office door opened again, and I looked up, expecting to see Dimitri.

But it was London.

Looking fucking beautiful in a strapless blue dress with straight hair. Her makeup was done like she had someplace to be. My cock immediately began to harden the second she entered the room, his thoughts on the ferocious way she needed me last night. She was horny as hell, and she needed me to fix it.

I was more than happy to oblige.

She walked up to my desk, strutting her hips like she was on a mission. She came around the glorious piece of furniture that had been there for hundreds of years and slid into my lap like she owned me and the entire room.

Dimitri hustled inside, out of breath. "I'm sorry, sir. I tried to stop her—"

I held up my hand and focused my gaze on her. "She's fine. Leave."

Dimitri darted out just as quickly as he came inside.

My hands moved to her thighs, my eyes focused on her green ones.

Her eyes were narrowed, and her shoulders were stiff like she had something to say to me. This wasn't just a visit about pleasure, even though she sat right on my hard-on. Her arms circled my neck, and she stared at me head on. "I don't want to share you with anyone."

I raised an eyebrow, not entirely sure what she meant.

"I want you to fuck me and only me." She spoke with a stern voice that matched her features, but it was adorable that this small woman was making demands. "I want it to be just the two of us. You give me what I need. I can give you whatever you need. No more late nights when you're out and about. I want you in that bed with me every night. End of story."

She didn't leave any room for negotiation, not that I had different terms in mind. She obviously thought I'd been fooling around with other women this entire time, when in reality, she was the only woman I'd even looked at. If this had been a few weeks ago, I would have pushed her off me and said her demands were ridiculous, that I would fuck whoever I wanted whenever I wanted.

But I didn't do that now.

I didn't hate the idea of monogamy. I didn't despise making any promise of fidelity to her. The fact that she wanted me all to herself caused a stirring in my pants. She made me feel needed, feel manly. She was my prisoner, but now we felt like partners, like she wanted to be there with me.

That was the sexiest thing of all.

This woman wanted me—badly.

I undid my belt and the top of my slacks as I kept my eyes on her. My hands reached for her dress next, and I yanked it up and pulled her panties to the side.

She reached behind her and grabbed the base of my cock and directed my length inside her. She slid all the way down to my balls, releasing a quiet moan as she moved.

I gripped her thighs and pressed my forehead against hers. "Just you and me."

"I made all the arrangements for the opening." Ariel sat in the armchair with her legs crossed, wearing a tight pencil skirt and a white blouse. She had a petite frame because she worked all day long and never ate anything. Sometimes, she drank scotch with me, but she usually preferred wine. "Caterers have been taken care of, everyone you invited RSVP'd, and we have the special wine you requested."

Did that mean Bones was coming? I'd have to give him a call to verify. "Josephine responded?"

"Yeah." She looked up from her folder with her black frames sitting on the bridge of her nose. She examined my expression, trying to read me. "Will that be a problem?"

I hadn't mentioned my current drama with my ex. "Yeah, it'll be fine. She stopped by last week, but I refused to see her. Then she called and told me her father had a heart attack." I told Ariel everything, so the words flowed. "She asked me to come over, but I told her not to call me again and hung up."

Ariel nodded with approval. "She can't have it both ways. She can't leave you and expect you to be there for her."

"I know." Ariel was just as cold as I was. That was probably why we got along so well.

"She has a lot of nerve, honestly."

"I agree."

When Ariel took a deep breath, I knew whatever she was going to say was tense. "So, are you bringing London, or did you have someone else in mind?" She made her feelings about my bedmate perfectly clear, so I knew what answer she was hoping for.

"London."

Ariel hardly hid her annoyance and scribbled in her notebook. "I'll arrange for her hair and makeup to be complete. I strongly encourage a short etiquette course. Her shoulders slouch, and she doesn't understand how to carry on a conversation with her superiors."

I smiled when I pictured how that conversation would go. That fire would leap in her eyes and burn indefinitely. "I'll run it by her."

"Good." She closed the folder. "That's all I have for now. If you need anything else, you know where to find me."

"I know. You never sleep." I gave her a smile and watched her rise out of the chair.

She still wore that stern expression, but she was fighting the smile that wanted to spread across her face. "Work comes first."

"Are you bringing someone to the opening?"

"Crewe, you know I never mix business with pleasure."

She didn't seem like someone who had a lot of pleasure in her life. "Well, you're always welcome to. You've met my women. I'd like to meet your men sometime—make sure they're good enough for you."

She finally smiled. "There's no man good enough for me." She walked out and left me alone in the office.

As usual, my thoughts returned to London. Whenever I was alone, she came into my thoughts. If Ariel knew I decided to share my bed with London exclusively, she wouldn't be too happy about it. Her fire would burn the entire castle.

I rubbed the scruff along my jaw and felt the urge to throw back a glass of scotch. I missed the burn all the way down my throat and into my stomach. But I was trying to cut back the way London asked me to, going from nine glasses a day to four. I'd already had one, so I needed to take a break before I moved on to the second glass. It was only noon.

I picked up the phone and called Bones, knowing that psychopath would stop me from thinking about the two drugs in my life.

"Crewe, how's the scotch business going?" He spoke with a deep voice that was just as rough as sandpaper. His tone made it sound like he was up to no good, a naturally sinister voice that was heavy with evil. I wondered if I sounded that way to other people.

"No complaints. How's the weapon business?"

"No complaints," he said with a chuckle. "To what do I owe the pleasure?"

I only bought weapons from Bones once before, and that was because the Barsetti brothers were unavailable. The craftsmanship was good and the quality was passable, but it was nothing compared to the product Crow and Cane offered. "I'm opening a second distillery in Edinburgh on Saturday night. Wanted to know if you're coming."

"I got your invitation. I might stop by. I'll be in the area anyway."

I chewed on the inside of my lip as I contemplated what to say next. Every move I made was just as strategic as a general moving warships out in the Atlantic Ocean. I wanted to know if he was bringing Vanessa, but I couldn't come out and ask. I shouldn't even know about Vanessa. "Hope to see you there."

"Will your pet be on your arm for the evening?"

All the muscles in my shoulders immediately tensed at the question. I didn't appreciate his tone, the way his breathing changed the second London was mentioned. Anger that I couldn't explain hovered at the surface under my skin, about to explode in a fiery combustion. "Yes. She's always on my arm."

He chuckled into the phone. "Looks like I missed out on an incredible woman. At least I found someone else to take her place."

I knew exactly who he was talking about. I swallowed my anger over London because that wasn't as important as my next question. "Will she be accompanying you on Saturday?"

"Possibly. We'll see how her bruises heal up."

I swallowed the bile that rose up my throat. I'd have to leave that comment out when I spoke to Crow. It would break him in half. "I look forward to meeting her."

"And I look forward to seeing your pet."

Before I could say anything to ruin things for Crow and Cane, I ended the conversation and got off the phone with him. I wasn't particularly close to the Barsetti brothers, but I understood what it was like to lose a family member. My offer to help them came from my own loss. If I at least had Alec, I might not feel so alone. I would have someone to share the burden of my name. I could have disappeared into the sunset and lived out my life in solitude along the coast of Greece. But I couldn't disgrace my parents' legacy by abandoning my duties.

I called Crow a few moments later. "Hey, it's Crewe."

"How's our product treating you?"

My men were happy to be armed with new equipment. The fortifications surrounding me reached a new peak. I kept a few guns for myself, stashing them in places that London wouldn't come across. "Well. Pristine, as usual."

"You get what you pay for. So, have you heard anything from him?" Crow rarely mentioned his name, always referring to him vaguely. He did a good job controlling his anger, but I thought I could feel his rage through the phone.

Maybe I was just imagining it. "I just got off the phone with him. He didn't give me a concrete answer, but he said he might stop by. And he said he might bring Vanessa."

Crow didn't say anything.

I gave him a moment to digest what I said. His mind was probably working a million miles an hour. If someone had been stolen from me, all I would ever think about was getting them back—along with my revenge. "You have a game plan in mind?"

"Cane and I will be there. We won't show our faces, and we'll remain out of sight. If we see an opportunity to grab her, we will."

"I'm sure he'll bring a few guards as well."

"We'll figure it out. Ideally, we'd like to make it seem like Vanessa ran for it. He won't suspect you that way."

"No gunshots, okay? There's gonna be a lot of important people there. My criminal activities are unknown to them, and it needs to stay that way."

"Understood. You're doing us a favor, and we wouldn't stab you in the back."

I took his word for it. "Thank you."

"I'll talk to you later."

I got off the phone then got back to work, resisting the glass of scotch I desperately wanted to drink.

I walked into the bedroom with my tie already loosened, anxious to see London since she hadn't made an appearance all day. Sometimes she came to my office for a visit, sitting on my lap and distracting me from the pile of work I needed to get through.

I wasn't ready for the sight I came upon. Standing in black lingerie, London looked like every man's fantasy. The lacy top had two openings where her tits hung freely, firm and perky with hard nipples. Her crotchless thong barely covered anything, leaving her long and beautiful legs visible for my eyes to cherish.

I'd never seen her in lingerie before. I'd never asked her to dress up for me, and now I was glad I never did. It was much more exciting when it was a surprise. I pulled my tie off my neck and slowly walked toward her as I dropped my jacket.

I took my time undressing in front of her, my eyes on her beautiful face the entire time. My throat went dry, and my heart raced in my chest. My cock was already hard from thinking about her all day, and now he was so thick he might burst.

I got my slacks and shoes off then dropped my boxers to the floor. My rock-hard dick greeted her with a distinct twitch. The fact that this woman wanted me so much when she used to despise me was such a turn-on. Now she needed me home every night, needed me inside her several times a day.

She circled my neck with her arms and kissed me hard on the mouth, her tongue diving past my lips with desperation. Her nails dug into me, razor-sharp and powerful. Her hands trailed down my body as she slowly lowered herself to her knees.

I took a deep breath when I knew what was coming next.

She grabbed the base of my cock and shoved my entire length inside her throat, her mouth gaping open and saliva pooling at the corners.

I already felt like a king in my own world. I owned everyone and everything. But nothing made me feel more kingly than having this woman on her knees with my cock in her mouth. Nothing made me feel more powerful than watching the desire burn in her eyes. My hand moved to the back of her neck, and I guided her up and down my length. Tears pooled in her eyes, and she struggled to breathe as my cock took up most of her throat. But she kept going because she knew I loved it— and she loved it too.

We had dinner on the balcony of the bedroom because London didn't want to go downstairs. She said she wanted to eat in my t-shirt and boxers, looking casual but sexy at the same time.

I preferred her in my clothes over a gown any day.

She cut into her fish and looked over the balcony, enjoying the lights from the rest of the castle and the cloudless sky. All the stars could be seen, twinkling high above us.

While she paid attention to the beauty surrounding us, I paid attention to her. Her mascara was slightly smeared because of the tears that had fallen from her eyes. Her hair was disheveled from the way I'd savagely gripped it. But all those imperfections made her flawless. She was more beautiful than any famous work of art that hung on my walls.

Our relationship was nothing compared how it used to be. It was a lot of bickering back and forth, my constant need to overpower her and restrain her every time she resisted. I had to conquer her more than once to get her to submit. But now there was a quiet companionship between us, a relationship full of silent conversations. I didn't have to put on a front with her anymore. She didn't need to put one on with me.

We could coexist—happily.

And the longer I had her in my life, the more beautiful I found her to be. Her features didn't change and her weight didn't fluctuate, but I found myself appreciating the curve of her cheekbones, the plumpness of her lips. I cared more about the beauty of her eyes than the shape of her figure. Her words had new meaning to them because I found everything she said insightful.

I didn't know what was happening, but I liked it.

She continued to eat quietly, her eyes downcast. There was a slight breeze in the air, and it blew a few strands away from her face.

I drank water with my meal, hating its blandness.

She looked across the table and noticed my nearly empty glass. "You've been doing well. I'm impressed."

"It hasn't been easy, but not impossible." It would be impossible for me to stop drinking altogether. That was something I wasn't willing to compromise on. But three to four glasses a day was doable.

"Feel any different?"

I could think more clearly and had a little more energy, but I was definitely moody. "I'm a little angry all the time."

She chuckled. "So nothing has changed."

I could resist the smile that formed on my face. "What did you do today?"

"I did Pilates in the living room. Then I hung up your clothes and cleaned everything."

"You know, I have maids for that."

"Well, I was bored. Running out of things to do."

I wanted to tell her she could always come visit me, but that would just slow down my workday. "You want a dog?"

"I can get a dog?" she asked in surprise.

"Why not?"

"Well, they're messy, and we travel a lot."

I shrugged. "Someone can take care of him."

"If I had a dog, I'd like to take care of him."

"Then maybe having a kid would be easier." The words flew out of my mouth without me thinking twice about it. I'd never considered having children with her. I'd never considered having her as anything more than just my bedmate.

She stared at me from across the table, her face unreadable. She wore a solid mask that hid her thoughts from view. She didn't seem repulsed by the idea, but she didn't seem happy about it either.

"I want to ask you something." I left my half-eaten plate on the table and kept my gaze focused on her.

"I'm listening."

"Am I the best you've ever had?" I suspected I already knew the answer based on the savage way she needed me all the time. But I wanted to hear her say it anyway, you know, because I was a sick egomaniac like that.

She swirled her wine before she took a drink, stalling as she thought of her answer.

I watched her intently the entire time, not blinking and sitting on the edge of my seat. If I asked her a personal question in the past, she usually dodged it. But now our relationship was a lot more relaxed. Conversations didn't feel like interrogations anymore.

She finally set down her glass. "You already know the answer."

"I want to hear it anyway."

Her eyes didn't flash with annoyance, not like they usually would. "Yes, you're the best I've ever had. Maybe that wasn't apparent after all the times you made me come, or all the times I asked you to fuck me in the middle of the night. You make the rest of the men I've been with look like boys. They didn't always make me come, probably because they didn't know what they were doing. I've never been kissed hard like that or ever felt more beautiful in my life. But with you, I've never felt more desirable." She grabbed her glass again and drank it like she hadn't just made the most erotic speech ever.

There was an invisible crown on my head, and I was staring at my queen. I gripped the armrests of my chair and wished there weren't dinner spread across the table. The maids would come and clean it at any moment. "You're the best I've ever had too."

This time when she looked at me, her expression was easy to read. She was surprised by my confession. "Really?"

"Yeah." She was different from any of the other women I'd been with. She was natural, real. She had a backbone of steel and a scowl that made grown men quiver. She was hard like a rock. "But you already knew that."

———

I sat up against the wooden headboard with my hands resting on her hips. My fingertips dug into her soft skin as I guided her up and down my length. She was rocking her hips slowly, taking my long length with restrained fluidness. She sheathed me to the balls then slowly rose up again, moving until only my thick head was inside her.

Her gorgeous tits were in my face, firm with hard nipples. Her petite shoulders led to a slender neck that had already been lavished with kisses. A quiet moan escaped her lips every time she took my entire length. Sometimes I would rock her back and forth, getting her clit stimulated against my muscular frame.

When she fucked me like this, I was in heaven.

When she rocked forward, her tits would move in my face. I would grace them with a kiss before I leaned back and watched her fuck me slowly. Her hands would glide up my chest to my shoulders, and she would use my body as an anchor so she could grind against me harder.

Goddamn.

My hands moved up her thighs, and I gripped her cheeks, squeezing the tight muscle in my palms. I was tempted to finger her asshole, but I suspected that would make me come sooner than I wanted.

Her breathing came out in short spurts, her moans cutting her off from the air that she needed. Her nails dug into me, and her eyes became lidded with intoxication. Our writhing bodies filled the room with the stench of sex.

I wanted to stay like this forever.

She rolled her head back then gripped her tits, squeezing them hard enough to make her wince.

Fuck.

She was slowly slipping away, diving headfirst into an orgasm that would make her toes curl. I'd fucked her enough times to pick up on her shallow breathing, the redness of her chest, and the way she swallowed every few seconds.

My hand moved between her legs, and I pressed my thumb to her throbbing clit. I rubbed it vigorously, making her hips buck automatically. I wanted a woman to enjoy me as much as I enjoyed her, but my primary focus with London was making her feel good. That felt better than having an orgasm. Sex had completely changed her perspective about being stuck with me. Now she needed me, relied on me. If the best way to keep her happy was satisfying her, I was more than happy to oblige.

Instantly, she ground herself against me and lost her breath altogether. Her hand clenched my wrist, and she moaned as the climax hit her. Her cunt tightened around my cock with a gripping force, and she came all over me, her delicious juice drenching my length. "Goddamn, Lovely..." I watched every expression she made, memorizing every detail because she was so stunning. Watching a woman come was always fun, but watching London come was a gorgeous sight. It was hard for me not to blow my load.

She gradually drifted back down to earth, her hips moving slowly over my length. Her breathing eventually returned to normal, and the redness on her chest faded away. She ran her hand through her hair, getting it off her sweaty neck. She had such a curvy figure, perky tits, an hourglass frame, and nice hips. She was so gorgeous it hurt.

Her grip slowly loosened on my wrist. "More."

My hands returned to her hips, and I clutched her hard. "As many times as you want, Lovely." It was my pleasure to satisfy this woman. There was nowhere else I'd rather be that night. I didn't want to call up Sasha or find a woman in a bar. The only woman I wanted to fuck was sitting on my lap at that very moment.

And that didn't scare me.

My hand moved up the center of her back until I reached the area just below her shoulder blades. I pulled her closer toward me so I could kiss her. My other hand still guided her up and down my length, needing to feel that wet pussy at the exact same time. My tongue circled hers, and the feel of her small mouth made my cock ache to explode. But I kept myself in line, taking my job as her lover very seriously.

I wanted to do this all night.

Losing sleep affected my workday and slowed my productivity. It was difficult for me to pay attention, and I had less energy to work out in the morning. But I wouldn't change anything because these were the nights I lived for. I was a king in my castle, and this gorgeous woman was my queen.

My scotch queen.

I washed off in the bathroom because I was so sweaty. I didn't mind the heat during sex, but once we were finished, I needed to feel cool. I pulled on a new pair of boxers and felt the sleep creep behind my eyelids. I had just had a powerful orgasm, pouring my come deep inside my woman, and now I was ready for bed.

I returned to the bed and saw her lying on her side of the bed, facing the window with her back to me. That was how she always slept, never crossing the invisible line in the center of the bed. She didn't snore, but I could tell when she was sleep. Her breathing was different, deep and gentle.

I got under the sheets and felt my eyes close immediately. With a bed this big, there was plenty of space for both of us. We never crossed paths in the middle of the night. Her legs didn't graze mine, and my hand never came into contact with hers.

It was nice.

But now I itched for something different. I loved feeling her soft skin against mine during sex, but I wanted to feel it more often than that. I wanted to my cock against her ass, her chest against my arm. I wanted to feel her body rise and fall with the breaths she took.

I crossed the invisible line and came to her side of the bed. My arm circled her waist, and I adjusted her against me, getting my cock in the crack of her cheeks and my chest right against her back. I could feel her breath, feel her pulse.

She stirred at the touch and looked at me over her shoulder, her eyes foggy like she was still asleep. Her arm circled mine, and she laid her head down again, going back to sleep without saying anything.

Being beside her was far more comfortable than sleeping alone. Every breath she took felt like a gentle lullaby. Her smell enveloped me and made my subconscious think of a field of flowers. I began to slip away immediately, dreaming of sunny skies with this beautiful woman beside me.

I didn't think of the people who betrayed me, my dead family, or the other bullshit going on in my life. When I was with her, all of that grief ceased to exist. It was just the two of us. It was the first sense of joy I'd had in a long time.

Maybe ever.

9

LONDON

My plan was working.

I didn't think he was in love with me yet, but he certainly felt something for me. The second he crossed that threshold and wrapped his arm around me, I knew our relationship had been taken to a whole new level.

I was anxious to test the waters.

I was anxious to get home and resume the life that had been taken away from me. I would be in a different semester in school by now. We would have moved on from the respiratory system and moved on to cardiology by now. I could have had a list of cardiac patients in the hospital that I was working with.

But I was here—trapped.

I could have had many normal conversations with my brother, talking about his bogus insurance job and my time in school. I could have gone out with my friends on Friday night as soon as our shift at the hospital ended. I never celebrated my birthday because no one in this new life even knew when it was.

He took all of that away from me.

A part of me felt bad for manipulating him like this, using sex and affection to make him see me as something more than just a possession, an act of revenge. But my brother's life was on the line, and my life had already been taken away from me. I was an innocent person living an ordinary life when he took all my hopes and dreams away.

I shouldn't feel bad at all.

I would judge myself for not doing everything possible to escape. To accept my fate would be pathetic and shameful. I only had one life to live, and I certainly wasn't going to spend it being Crewe's prisoner.

I deserved to be free, for god's sake.

I needed to organize a plan and find a solution to this problem. The only way I could do that would be to communicate with Joseph, but I had no way of doing that.

Unless I asked Crewe if I could call him.

He might say yes if I played my cards right.

It was worth a shot.

I sat in the southern garden and looked across the hillsides to the mountains beyond. Even though we were just minutes from the city, from this view, it seemed like we were in the middle of nowhere.

I was so far away from home.

The sun was setting so it was almost dark. Dinner would probably be ready soon, and Crewe would be looking for me, expecting to see me in the bedroom where I waited for him every day like a dog.

He eventually found me sitting on the stone bench in the garden. He'd already showered and changed into jeans and a t-shirt, looking just as sexy as he did when he was in his suit. All my actions were geared toward manipulating him, but I'd be lying if I said I didn't enjoy it. The sex was amazing. I wasn't lying when I said he was the best I'd ever had. I'd never met a man more beautiful in my life.

He didn't say a word as he took the seat beside me, his brown eyes on me.

I leaned toward him and gave him a soft kiss on the mouth, a sensual one that lacked tongue. It was slow but purposeful. When I pulled away, I could tell he didn't want the kiss to end. I moved to his side on the bench and admired the view.

His arm draped over the back of the chair, his fingertips touching my shoulder. "What are you doing out here, Lovely?"

"I came out here a while ago and lost track of time…"

His hand moved to the back of my head, and he gently touched my hair, his fingers working my scalp. Affectionate touches like that were becoming more frequent. He stopped grabbing me by the neck when he wanted something and treated me like a human being. "Something on your mind?"

There was my opportunity. "Kinda. It's nothing important, and I don't want to bore you with it."

His fingers stopped moving in my hair. Instead, he grabbed the back of my head with his fingertips and gently shifted my face toward him. "You could never bore me, Lovely. Tell me."

He never told me anything, but I didn't bring that up. I got him to stop seeing other women, which was already a big gesture, so I couldn't be too picky. "I guess I miss my brother. It's his birthday…and I always call him on his birthday." That was all bogus. It wasn't his birthday, but Crewe probably didn't know that. I kept looking over the fields without expressing any expectation. I didn't want to outright ask if I could call him. It'd be much easier if Crewe showed some compassion and made the offer on his own.

Crewe didn't say anything at all. His fingers moved through my hair again.

Damn. Was it stupid of me to actually think it would be that easy? "How was work?"

Crewe moved to the back of my neck and massaged the muscle, his thumb and forefinger powerful. Anytime he touched me, he always made me feel good. When his touch was sexual, it always lit me on fire. When it was comforting, it made me feel incredible. "You can call him." He pulled his phone out of his pocket and pulled the number on the screen. Then he handed it over to me.

Oh my god. It actually worked.

I stared at the phone without taking it, my eyebrow raised. "What?"

He continued to hold it. "I'll give you ten minutes. Here."

I finally took the phone, feeling my hand shake. "You're being serious?"

"Yeah. It's not like there's anything either of you can do anyway."

I stared at my brother's number but didn't press send. Now that I actually got my way, I didn't know what to do. "Can I have some privacy?"

Crewe stared me down, his expression unreadable.

"You just said neither one of us can do anything…"

Crewe considered my words before he finally nodded. "Ten minutes. Not a second longer." He leaned into me and kissed me on the mouth before he left the bench, his shoulders tense and his posture rigid. He carried himself with perfect grace every second of the day. Even if he went to the bathroom in the middle of the night, he still held himself like a soldier.

When he walked inside, I was still frozen in shock. That went over way easier than I expected. It almost seemed like a trick, but there was no way it could be unless Crewe had expected me to do this from the beginning.

I remembered my ten minutes were running, so I hit send and press the phone to my ear. It rang as I realized the balcony of our bedroom overlooked this courtyard. Crewe could be watching me, and if I spoke too loudly, he could hear me.

Joey answered. "Crewe." He spoke with a voice pregnant with hate. I'd never heard that tone in his voice before. Even when we fought as kids, that kind of unbridled rage never made an appearance.

"It's London. He said I have ten minutes to talk to you."

"London?" His voice completely changed when he realized it was me. "He let you call me?"

"Yeah. He's not around. I can speak freely."

"Don't be so sure. He's not stupid."

I was certain I really had the privacy I asked for. I think Crewe trusted me, on some level. "No, we're alone."

"Why would he let you speak to me alone?"

"Because I've been working on what we last talked about." No need to spell it out if Joseph knew what I was talking about. "I think I've made a lot of progress. Things are different. I don't know how much longer this is going to take me, but we're definitely on the right track."

This was awkward for Joseph. No easy way to discuss the fact that his little sister was being fucked every night by the guy who captured her. Joseph had always been protective of me since we lost our parents, and I knew he felt all the guilt of the entire situation. "Well…that's good. You think he'll eventually let you go?"

"I don't know…maybe." I wasn't sure how long that would take to happen. Once I asked for my freedom, all my cards would be on the table. He would know everything between us was just a lie. "But I think I could at least ask for him to turn off the transmitter in your head for good. That wouldn't be unreasonable."

"London, I don't care about that. I care about you."

My eyes immediately watered at the sincerity in his voice. My captivity was killing him every single day. We were ripped apart when we were all we had left of our family. "Well…that's the best we can do for now." I did my best to keep the emotion out of my voice.

"We're gonna have to do something else, possibly a takedown."

"A takedown?"

"I'm going to have to round up all my men and any extras I can find and ambush him. Kill everyone, including him. That's the only way we both walk free."

It sounded logical, but the idea of all the bloodshed made me uneasy. And as lame as it was, I didn't want Crewe to die. He deserved to be killed for what he'd done to me since I was an innocent person, but I still couldn't do it. "I'll keep working with him and see if I can make it happen. I'd rather do that than have you risk your life."

"I don't care about that either, London. I've got to get you out of there. It kills me…"

"I know," I whispered. "But it's really not that bad. He treats me well."

"You would say that even if it weren't true."

"But it is true," I said. "I'm not defending Crewe because he's a bad man…but he does have compassion, empathy, and a heart. I've seen it myself. If he really were evil, he would have given me to Bones. I prefer Crewe any day."

Joseph stayed quiet, still not believing me.

I couldn't come out and say Crewe and I were having amazing sex, that our chemistry was scorching and I trusted him to take care of me. So I didn't say anything more about it. "Crewe is having a grand opening for his distillery in Edinburgh. It sounds like there's gonna be a lot of people there. Maybe we can cross paths."

"I can make it happen. I know the area you're referring to. Shouldn't be too difficult."

"Don't get caught. If you do, it'll blow everything for me."

"I won't," he said with confidence. "I'll think of a plan over the week. Maybe I can get you out of there that night."

"Out of there?" I asked. "There's no way you can take me away without him killing you."

"But you said he's been falling for you."

"Yeah…so what?"

"Maybe he won't do it. Maybe he won't have the balls to hit the trigger."

In most instances, Crewe was an honorable guy. He was helping Crow and Cane get their sister back even though he didn't owe them anything, and he took care of me every single day. There was a good chance he wouldn't do it. But when Crewe was pissed off…there was no telling what he might do. "I'm not willing to take that chance."

"Well, I am. I'd much rather die than let him keep you any longer."

Maybe this phone call was a bad idea. "I'm not going with you, so don't bother."

"You don't have a choice, London. If I see a chance to get you out of there, I'm gonna take it."

"No." Joseph was more stubborn than I was. When he put his mind to something, he never changed it. "We aren't doing that. We'll figure something else out. I just need a little more time with him, and I can make things happen."

"There's no way to know if he'll go that soft. I honestly don't think he ever will. He has too much pride. This is our only choice."

"Joseph, no. If you come for me, I won't cooperate."

"I'll make you cooperate. You're all the family I have left, London. I'm not letting that piece of shit touch you any longer."

I couldn't let this happen. "If this plan backfires and you die, then I would have spent six months with this man for no reason. All my time would have been wasted. That can't be an option."

"London, this is all we have. This is our one shot, and I'm willing to take a gamble on this guy."

I wanted to scream. "You took a gamble on him the first time, and look where we ended up."

Joseph didn't have a comeback for that.

"And when someone crosses him, he doesn't sweep it under the rug. He'll never forget it. I don't think we can rely on his compassion for this. Our best hope is for me to talk to him when I think he's ready."

Joseph was quiet over the line as he considered what he said. "You're aren't risking anything. I'm getting you out of there. End of story."

"Joseph—"

"I'll see you on Saturday."

"Joseph!"

He hung up.

When the line went dead against my ear, I knew he was gone. The blood drained from my face when I realized the mess I'd gotten myself into. I never should have called him. I should have known he would risk his life to get me away from Crewe. I underestimated him.

Crewe walked into the courtyard at that moment, announcing the end of my ten minutes.

I pretended my brother was still on the line. "Well, I have to go. I'll talk to you later."

Crewe sat on the bench beside me and draped his arm over the back of the chair.

"Love you too." I pulled the phone from my ear and acted like I hit the end button. Now I had to pretend that I didn't just get myself into a nightmare. Joseph was organizing his own plan to sneak me out of the opening, but I wasn't sure if Crewe was as soft as I hoped he was. If he did feel something for me, he might be ticked that I was taken away. I really had no idea.

I handed the phone back. "Thanks for letting me call him."

"Yeah." He dropped it into his pocket. "Didn't see the harm."

There was a lot of harm in it, actually.

"I might let you call him again sometime."

"That would be nice."

"What did you guys talk about?"

Nothing I could share. "He told me he had a date the other night. Said he liked her, but it could never go anywhere...because of what he does. It was the first time we've ever spoken and he was honest with me. Kinda feels like I'm talking to another person."

Crewe nodded like he understood. "It must be a drastic change."

"Insurance salesman..." I shook my head. "I should have known that was bogus. Too boring for a guy like him."

"I don't know about that," he said. "If someone wants to hide something, they will."

"So what exactly happened with the two of you?" I knew the basics, not the specifics.

"He crossed me," he said coldly. "That's about it."

"What intelligence did he want?"

"He wanted to know more about the leader of Austria. He never told me why."

I couldn't wrap my mind around that. Joseph was involved in criminal affairs. He bought intelligence for millions of dollars and used it in horrible ways. It was like I didn't know my brother at all.

"We made the deal. He brought the money, and my men brought the paperwork. I didn't check the money because I think it's rude to assume you're making a deal with a crook. But an hour later, I realized the bills were fake. And that's when I launched my attack." He stared across the courtyard and into the darkness up ahead. The lights from the castle allowed us to see the stone walkways and flowers. "I can't let people get away with stuff like that. People talk. Everyone in my universe knows I've taken you as payment. Now no one else will fuck with me."

I shook my head. "What did he think was gonna happen? That you weren't gonna notice?"

He shrugged. "Possibly thought I wouldn't notice for a day or two. And he assumed he would be off the radar so I couldn't find him again. Ironically, I was never planning on going after him. I'm a man who finds information, and it didn't take long for me to find out about you. Stupid mistake on his part." His hand returned to the back of my hair, and he massaged my scalp with his fingertips. "But I think I came out ahead in the deal. You're worth more than four million dollars."

It was a sweet thing to say in a very twisted way.

He turned my face in his direction and leaned in to kiss me. It was full of affection and kindness rather than possession. That was how he always kissed me, with gentleness. "Ready for dinner?"

It took a second for me to answer the question because that kiss was still heavy in my mind. "Yeah…" I leaned in farther and kissed him again, wanting more of that affection he lavished me with. Letting me call my brother was a compassionate thing to do, especially since my intentions were anything but innocent. I felt a twinge of guilt for what I had done, especially since Joseph was moving forward with a plan I never agreed to.

Crewe kissed me back with the same passion, his hand gliding up my neck until his thumb rested just behind my ear. "You wanna skip dinner?"

"No, I'm starving. But let's postpone it."

He smiled against my mouth. "Sounds good to me."

I crawled on my hands and knees on the bed and looked at him over my shoulder.

He moved on top of me and pressed his chest to my back, his skin warm and his physique powerful. His lips moved down my neck until they found my mouth. He kissed me hard as he rubbed his cock between my ass cheeks.

My pussy was soaked, and I was eager for him to be inside me. I loved his kisses and his caresses, but the foreplay had gone on long enough. I didn't need much to get my engine revving, not when it came to Crewe.

He grabbed my shoulder, rolled me to my back, and moved between my legs. His hands pinned mine to the mattress on either side of my head, and his hips separated my knees.

I'd assumed he wanted my ass in his face, but he quickly changed the dynamic.

He read the question in my eyes. "I love watching you come." He wrapped my legs around his hips and made my ankles lock together. His body returned to mine, and he slid his cock inside me without opposition, my channel slick and wet, but also tight.

"Oh god…" My hands reached out to his chest for support the second I felt him stretch me. I saw stars in my eyes, and my breathing quickened instantly. I squeezed my thighs around his hips, and my nails dug into him slightly.

He rocked into me slowly, his eyes on me the entire time. "I've never seen anything so beautiful in my life." His mocha colored eyes were darker in the dimly lit bedroom, but the passion was burning brighter than ever before. He looked like a king as he held himself with ease on top of me, the beads of sweat starting at his temples.

"Crewe…" The confession went straight to my heart. He wasn't the same man that I met when I first came into his captivity. He was coarse and sarcastic, empty and rude.

He never had anything even somewhat pleasant to say, and now all those walls of malcontent had disappeared. He made sure no one ever laid a hand on me, and he never hurt me himself. I was the only woman in his bed because he wanted me to be the only one. I'd accomplished the impossible and knew it was an impressive feat. But in that instant, I didn't care about my success. I cared about the moment I shared with him, the feeling of our bodies moving together in perfect harmony. I loved every inch of him, and there was never a time I felt more connected to him than when we were fucking.

Or making love.

My arms circled his neck, and I pulled his lips to mine for a kiss. My tits rubbed against his muscular chest, feeling the light amount of curly hair brush against my soft skin. I could feel his sweat, the strength of his body.

His tongue moved in my mouth, never overstaying its welcome as it moved with mine. He retracted his tongue then kissed my lips again, feeling them with purpose. His kiss was never predictable, never the same. He always moved with his passion, giving me a different kind of affection every time he embraced. I could feel his arousal, the way I turned him on when we touched.

And that turned me on in a whole new way.

"I want your come," I whispered against his mouth, wanting to feel that heavy weight of seed deep inside me. I wanted to sleep with his essence sitting inside my body all night long.

He moaned against my mouth and kept moving.

I didn't need to come twice tonight. I was satisfied from the way he took me earlier in the day. Now I just wanted us to both find our release at the same time, to feel that ecstasy that we gave one another.

He changed his thrusts and ground against my clit with his movements, trying to bring me to orgasm as quickly as possible. He sucked my bottom lip into his mouth as his breathing quickened, the headboard tapping against the wall in a rhythm that matched his pace.

His expression darkened, and his jaw tensed, fighting the pleasure that started deep in his core. He was fighting off an orgasm, trying to edge himself until I could cross the finish line before him.

Seeing him fight his pleasure only increased mine. He was the sexiest man I'd ever been with, making me explode with every touch he gave. When I slept beside him every night, I knew nothing would ever happen to me. I felt safer with him than anywhere else in the entire world.

"I'm gonna come…"

"Yes, Lovely." He rocked into me harder.

It hit me hard, like a train crashing into a brick building. My hands dug into his shoulders, and I released a restrained scream. His cock hardened inside me as I constricted around him, and I was hit with different waves of pleasures. I writhed and moaned, loving how incredible he made me feel. "Crewe…" I dug my fingers into his ass and pulled him harder into me, still feeling the remains of the blinding orgasm. Now I wanted to feel his come.

He gave a few swift pumps before he reached his threshold. He buried himself deep inside me and released with a loud moan. His expression hardened as his eyes focused on me. His jawline was tight, and all the muscles in his body flexed as the euphoria swept through him. "Lovely…" He deposited everything he had inside my channel, filling me with the mounds of come I was used to getting before we went to sleep.

My fingers returned to his hair as I kissed him, silently thanking him for giving me the most incredible orgasm to date. My lips treasured the corner of his mouth and everywhere else, even the stubble on his chin.

He moved his face into the valley of my breasts and kissed the sweat away, his lips sucking each of my nipples into his mouth and giving them a playful nibble. He pulled his softening cock out, leaving his deposit behind.

He got off me and lay on his back beside me, his chest rising and falling from his heavy breathing. He stared at the ceiling with his hand resting on his chest.

I moved to the other side and immediately felt sleepy. I never skipped a meal, but now I couldn't care less about eating. I was so comfortable where I was, my eyes fluttering as sleep overtook me.

Minutes later, Crewe moved to my side of the bed and spooned me from behind. His actions had become predictable, and I was used to feeling his arms around me while we slept all night.

I turned around and faced him, my arm circling his neck and my leg hooking around his waist.

His hand wrapped around my waist, and he pulled me closer to him, making sure there wasn't an inch of empty space between us. We were stuck together like glue, becoming one person with our bodies wrapped around one another. "No dinner tonight?"

I sighed. "Too tired."

"I'm too comfortable to move anyway."

I closed my eyes and felt the cloud of sleep instantly descend. I was slipping away into the darkness, my body relaxing from the way Crewe kept me warm. I felt his lips brush against my forehead before he planted a kiss just above the middle of my eyebrows. His lips were warm and wet, and the embrace lasted for seconds.

Now I was awake again, warmed by the unexpected affection he gave me. Joy radiated through me when I realized I accomplished something I never thought was possible. But then the guilt quickly followed afterward. The more Crewe softened for me, the more I softened for him. I felt loyalty to this man when I shouldn't feel anything. I felt jealousy when I shouldn't care where he was or who he was with.

I felt everything when I shouldn't feel anything.

10

CREWE

"Crewe, you have a moment?" Ariel poked her head inside my office.

"I always have a moment for you."

She smiled and walked inside, looking elegant in her tight skirt and blouse. She always looked perfectly manicured every time I saw her. Even when I needed something from her in the middle of the night, she looked as elegant as a queen. "Have I ever told you you're my favorite boss?" She sat down and crossed her legs.

"No. But I assumed. What's up?"

"I have the hairdresser and makeup artist lined up for London." The second she was mentioned, Ariel's mood soured. "And I strongly encourage the etiquette course. Should I set that up as well?"

I knew London would never go for it. Besides, she was perfect the way she was. "That won't be necessary."

Ariel made the note without objection, but her jaw tightened in annoyance. "Very well. And you're still certain you want to take her? There's going to be a lot of respectable people there."

I'd assured Ariel nothing serious was going on between London and me. In fact, I gave her my word. But now everything was changing, and I wasn't even sure what was going on. It would be easier to take Sasha or someone else, but I didn't want another woman on my arm. London wouldn't want that either. "Yes, I'm certain."

Ariel hid her annoyance again, but I knew her so well that it was obvious she was ticked.

"You should bring someone, Ariel. It's a social function, after all." I never met any of the men in her life. She never talked about her personal life, even when I asked questions. I understood her need for professionalism, but we were still friends. I cared about her as a person, not just a business partner.

"I may."

"That's great. I'd love to meet him."

She only smiled in response.

"I might give him a bit of an interrogation, but I'm sure he can handle it. If he's with you, he must be pretty solid."

Her smile didn't drop. "We'll see." She rose from the chair, standing on her heels with an ease that implied she was barefoot. "Need anything else?"

"No, I don't think so."

"You know where to find me." She walked out and closed the door behind her.

My thoughts turned to London once I was alone. That woman was on my mind constantly, even when I was in the middle of a business meeting. Like a cloud that hung over my head, she followed me everywhere I went.

Letting her speak to her brother was an impulse decision. Maybe I would regret it later, but I suspected I wouldn't. He thought his life could be claimed at any point in time when my thumb decided to hit the trigger. London would never jeopardize her brother's life, and Joseph wouldn't cross me again.

I wondered if the threat on Joseph's life wasn't the only reason London was with me.

That she wanted to be with me.

Every time we were together, it seemed different. She wanted me all to herself, she wanted me to spend all of her free time with me, and she looked at me like I was the only man in the world who mattered.

I wondered if her feelings had grown from hatred, to lust…and to something more.

I was afraid the same had happened to me.

I told myself that would never happen because it didn't seem possible. My heart had been broken and humiliated, and I was too angry to feel anything besides spite. But I cut back on drinking, stopped seeing other women, and London was the only thing I thought about exclusively.

How did I get here?

Dimitri knocked on the door and popped his head inside. "Sir, may I come in?"

"Yes." I didn't miss Dunbar at all. Ever since he'd been put on tower duty, he hadn't had any conflicts with London. It was an easy fix.

Dimitri approached my desk with an envelope in hand. "London asked me to give this to you."

"Lady London," I corrected as I took the envelope from him.

He nodded his head. "My apologies, sir." He walked out and shut the door behind him.

I examined the letter and had no idea what she was up to. Why send me a letter when she could just come down here and speak to me? I preferred our conversations when she was sitting right on my lap.

I ripped open the sleeve and pulled out the small piece of paper that had been ripped from a pad of stationery. A single sentence was written in her feminine handwriting.

Sir,

Come upstairs and fuck me in the ass.

-Lovely-

` . .

I stared at the paper and felt my hand shake. My fingers grew numb, and I dropped the sheet on my desk, my pants suddenly feeling tight from the sentence I just read. It was quickest I'd ever gotten hard in my life.

I left the desk instantly, refusing to keep my woman waiting.

I finished donning my black suit, one of my most expensive ones that I reserved for special occasions. Everything I wore was nice and designer quality, but some of the finer things were always kept in special storage. I didn't even expose those outfits to air for fear of fading or wrinkling.

I looked at myself in the mirror and adjusted my tie for the last time. My appearance wasn't just important because of the royalty who would see me. The only opinion I really cared about was London's. Sometimes she looked at me with desperation in her eyes, her hands usually pressed hard into my chest. She was turned on with just a single look.

I liked that.

I walked down the hall and entered our bedroom where London was getting ready. We had to leave soon, so she should be almost finished.

When I walked inside, she was just as beautiful as I expected. The dress fit her perfectly, as it had when she'd first tried it on in Italy. It reached the floor and covered her heels, and it fit her bust like it was made for her. Her slender shoulders were round and led to a graceful neck that had been smothered with countless kisses. Her hair was pulled back with two small braids intertwined with her hair. A diamond necklace hung around her throat, and her makeup was done to highlight her features subtly. A beautiful woman like her didn't need much makeup anyway.

I admired her from the doorway and watched the hairdresser make the final adjustments. He looked at her reflection in the mirror and nodded in approval. "You'll outshine the Queen."

"What?" she blurted. "The Queen is going to be there?"

"According to her assistant, she is." I stepped into the room and came to London's side, unable to take my eyes off her. She looked exactly the same as she did during Holyrood week, but to me, she looked like a whole new person. My arm circled her waist, and my lips moved to her ear. "You look perfect."

Her features melted, and a smile formed on her lips. "I like your suit." Just as I hoped, her hand moved to my chest. It was the clear-cut sign that she wanted me, that if we were alone together, my pants would be around my ankles.

I pulled her into me and kissed her hairline. "Thank you, Lovely. Are you ready to go?"

"Yeah…" Her bright features suddenly softened. "I think so."

I noticed her unease immediately. "What is it, Lovely?"

She broke eye contact. "Nothing."

The hairdresser silently excused himself so we could be alone together.

I turned her toward me, forcing her to meet my gaze. "Tell me." There was nothing she couldn't say to me. I was patient and understanding. I showed her more compassion than I'd shown anyone in my life.

"I don't want to see him, that's all."

I knew exactly whom she was talking about. "You have nothing to be afraid of."

Her eyes moved down again.

"Look at me."

She took a deep breath before she met my gaze.

"You know I would never let anyone touch you. Right?"

She nodded.

"You know I would never let anyone ever make you feel uncomfortable. So relax."

"Okay," she whispered.

I kissed the corner of her mouth. "Then let's go."

11

LONDON

Man, my heart was racing.

It thumped in my chest sporadically, pounding hard against my rib cage and nearly making me shake. I sat in the back seat of the black car with Crewe beside me, my large dress taking up the chair and the floor. When I arrived, I didn't know what to expect. Joseph would be waiting to make his move, and the monster that haunted my dreams would be there as well.

I didn't know what to do.

I couldn't be alone, even for a minute. If Crewe excused himself to use the restroom or to speak to someone

266 | PENELOPE SKY

important in private, I would have to cling to his side anyway. If I had to pee, I would be forced to hold it. If Joseph got me alone, I would be powerless to stop him.

So I had to make sure Crewe never left my side.

This night was gonna be long.

Crewe held my hand on his thigh, his piercing gaze examining my face. "You're flushed."

"Just nervous."

"You've done this once before."

"Doesn't make it any easier. You never get nervous to entertain a room full of the most important people in the world?"

He shrugged. "I'm used to it. I've been doing this sort of thing for over thirty years."

"Well, I haven't. How am I supposed to introduce myself?"

He smiled. "You remember your name, don't you?"

"I mean, what am I to you?"

"No one will ask."

"Uh…I think they might. I can't say I'm your girlfriend."

"Why not?" he asked with furrowed eyebrows.

"I didn't think dukes had girlfriends. Don't they just choose someone to marry, and that's it?"

His expression didn't change. "We live in modern times now. If it comes up, you're my girlfriend."

I was? "Okay."

The travel to Edinburgh was painfully quick. We got there in no time at all. My heart was still pounding in my chest, and I wanted a time machine just to get through the night as quickly as possible. I wanted to avoid Bones and my brother without getting stuck with some duke from Iceland in the corner, talking about politics I didn't understand. I was glad Crewe took me as his date because I obviously meant something to him, but I'd much rather be at the castle waiting for him to come home. "Ariel didn't have a problem with you taking me?" It was the one time I relied on her to help me. I knew she hated me and would have done anything possible to prevent this from happening. But she dropped the ball on that.

"I don't care if she had a problem." He kept his eyes out the window. "She's just my business partner. Her opinion about my personal life is irrelevant."

Damn.

We arrived at the distillery minutes later. We were an hour early before the party actually began, probably because it was customary for the host to greet the guests as they arrived.

Crewe helped me out of the car and circled his arm around my waist as he guided me inside. The place was constructed of stone-white and brown bricks, and the trees outside were covered in white lights. In my mind, I was picturing a warehouse of some kind. But this place was beautiful.

We walked inside to see a beautifully decorated hall. It could easily fit a hundred people, and I wondered what was usually stored inside. I imagined there were barrels of scotch everywhere, ready to be shipped to large businesses or wealthy clients. Waiters and workers were still preparing everything, and Crewe dropped his hand from my waist to give further instruction.

It was starting.

I immediately moved to his side and stuck to him like glue, taking a step every time he did. There was no way I was going to be left alone, even for a second. Joseph could be watching me at that very moment.

Waiting for the perfect opportunity.

12

CREWE

The party was in full swing, and everyone seemed to be having a good time. I greeted the Queen at the entrance, and she remembered London from the first time they met. Despite her old age, she was as sharp as a tack and refined as ever.

I introduced London to other members of the nobility, and she smiled and remained polite. She hardly said anything other than pleasantries, probably because she was so nervous. I'd rarely seen London show her unease when she was out of her comfort zone, but she was definitely showing her vulnerability tonight.

When I had a moment to breathe, I guided London to the side and waited for a waiter to appear with a tray of wine. "You're doing great, Lovely."

"I am?" she whispered. "Because I feel utterly terrified right now."

"What's there to be scared of?" My hand was glued to her waist because I wanted everyone in the room to know she was mine. She wasn't just my friend or an employee. She was the woman sleeping in my bed every night.

"Uh, are you kidding?" she asked. "I just met the Queen —again. How many people can say that?"

"A lot of Brits, actually. She makes a lot of public appearances."

"That's like me meeting the President of the United States. It's unbelievable."

Her reverence was cute, and I couldn't help but smile. "If it makes you feel better, I can barely tell you're nervous. You're doing great."

"It's because I downed a whole glass of scotch when we walked inside."

"Well, there's always more if you need it." I'd been good at cutting back every day. I managed to get by with three glasses of scotch instead of nine. It was hard in the beginning, but it got easier as time went on. I actually felt better because of the change.

"I may take you up on that offer."

I glanced at the door and saw Josephine walk inside with Sir Andrew. He wore a deep navy blue suit and stood a foot taller than her. With features typical of the Irish nobility, he had bright blond hair and searing blue eyes. He was ten years older than her and not really as good-looking as me.

But she made her choice.

Josephine's eyes landed on me, and she stared at me without blinking.

After that night when she called me, I didn't think about her again. My thoughts had been filled with London exclusively.

But my duty required me to greet both of them. The best way to kill scandal was to absorb it. By inviting them to my gatherings and being civil to them, it made the fiasco look less dramatic. But it was all an act.

I hated both of them.

I guided London with me as I approached the happy couple. Andrew's arm was around Josephine's waist, and she wore a cream-colored dress with a red shawl. She looked like typical royalty. I could spot her in a crowd instantly. "Good evening. Thank you for coming." As customary, I kissed Josephine on the hand even though I'd rather throw up on it.

Josephine watched my movements, the sadness in her eyes.

I shook Andrew's hand next, pretending this interaction was perfectly normal. "Great to see you."

"The pleasure is ours," Andrew said with his Irish accent. "I can already tell it's going to be a night to remember. Congratulations on your success, Crewe."

I didn't care how polite he was. I still hated the bastard. "Thank you. Have you met London?" I squeezed her into my side.

"No, I haven't." Andrew looked at her just the way I did, like her beauty was impossible to mistake. "Lovely to meet you." He shook her hand. "I'm sorry, what is your title?"

London eyed me as if she didn't know what to say.

"She's my girlfriend," I said. "She's an American doctor who recently moved here."

I knew London would argue that wasn't true since she never received her license, but it was the quickest way to explain her hobbies.

Josephine's face immediately paled when she realized what London meant to me. Her eyes dropped, and her mind drifted away from the conversation as the truth hit her hard.

"That's lovely," Andrew said. "Welcome to Scotland. I'm sure you'll love it."

"I already do," London answered.

Andrew returned his hand to Josephine's waist and guided her away to join the rest of the festivities.

London released the breath she was holding and looked at me when we were alone again. "Is that the same Josephine who came to the house a few months ago?"

The question was pretty much rhetorical because she already knew the answer. "Yes."

London watched Josephine join the crowd with Andrew, her eyes glued to every movement she made. "She loves you. I can tell just by looking at her." She turned to me for confirmation.

I didn't like keeping secrets from London anymore. It was easier to be honest with her since I was sharing my entire life with her. She was there every second of the day, sharing my bed every second of the night. "She does. But I don't love her anymore."

She couldn't hide the surprise on her face when I shared something so personal with her. Her eyebrows were high, and she parted her lips in a sexy way. The braid that was pinned up with the rest of her hair made her look more graceful than usual. She was by far the most beautiful woman in the room that night. "So you used to be together…"

"Yeah. It ended about a year ago." I didn't get into the specifics just in case someone was eavesdropping. I couldn't exactly call Josephine a cunt when someone else could overhear it and rat me out. Wasn't good decorum.

"Oh…" A red tint came into her cheeks, and her expression slowly hardened with every passing second. I'd seen that look a few times and knew exactly what it meant. She was jealous—very jealous. She glanced at Josephine before she looked at me. She came closer into my chest then rose on her tiptoes to kiss me, probably hoping Josephine would see.

I didn't care if Josephine was looking or not. When my woman kissed me, all I cared about doing was kissing her back. My hands gripped her petite waistline, and I didn't care about the public display of affection we were showing everyone. It wasn't classy or appropriate, but I still didn't care.

When my cock hardened in my slacks, I pulled away before I could get carried away. When we were back in the car on the drive home, she was going to straddle my hips and fuck me in the back seat. But that was a few hours away, so I shouldn't get too excited.

I spotted Ariel walk inside the front door wearing a skintight black dress with matching heels. Her hair was curled, and she looked ready to have a good time, not sit around and work. Her glasses didn't sit on the bridge of her nose, and her dark hair looked good with everything she wore. "I'm going to say hello to Ariel." I knew London would want nothing to do with my business partner. They simply couldn't get along, and it was easier just to accept it than to force them to play nice.

London grabbed my hand and pressed herself into my side. "I'll come with you."

"Are you sure? You can mingle with everyone else."

"No, I don't want to leave your side." She pressed closer into me, her breasts rubbing against my ribs.

Hearing her need me was sexy, so I pulled her along with me and walked up to Ariel. It wasn't until I was up close that I spotted the other woman with her. Blond, petite, and beautiful, she was close enough to Ariel that their shoulders touched.

It only took a few seconds for me to figure it out.

"You look beautiful tonight, Ariel." I leaned into her and pressed a kiss to her cheek.

"Thanks, Crewe. You look nice too." Ariel looked at London and gave her the fakest smile in the world. Then she turned back to me. "This is Cassandra. Cassandra, this is the man I'm always telling you about."

Cassandra smiled brighter than the stars then kissed me on the cheek. She hugged London, being far nicer to her than Ariel ever was. She had the complete opposite personality, full of buoyancy and playfulness. "It's so nice to meet you both of you. Ariel talks about you all the time. You know her, it's always about work."

Ariel rolled her eyes. "It's not *always* about work."

Cassandra gave her a firm look full of disagreement.

Ariel shrugged it off.

"Can I get you ladies something to drink?" I asked.

"Nonsense," Cassandra said. "I can handle that. I'm sure you two want to catch up. You want to come with me, London?"

London clutched my hand with an ice-cold grip. "Uh, I'm okay. Thank you, though."

Cassandra didn't care about the brush-off and walked away.

Now that I was alone with Ariel, I felt like I should apologize. "I'm sorry that I made any assumptions before." I constantly assumed she had boyfriends in her life. If I paid more attention, I probably would have picked up on the subtle hints she dropped.

"You don't need to apologize, Crewe." Ariel was always right to the point, borderline heartless. It was nearly impossible to offend her because she didn't give a damn about anyone's opinion, another reason why I liked her so much. "We've been seeing each other for a few months. I met her in London. She's wonderful."

I smiled, feeling happy that she had someone. It seemed like she was working all the time, slaving away over the scotch business and my other forms of revenue. I didn't want her to revolve her entire universe around work like I did. There was more to life. "She's lovely. She balances you well."

Ariel grinned. "Because she's pleasant?"

"Because she's a little more laid-back. Maybe she'll teach you how to relax."

Ariel chuckled. "She definitely does that."

Cassandra returned with two glasses of wine and handed one to Ariel.

"Thanks, honey." Ariel kissed her on the cheek then took a drink. "We're going to say our pleasantries. Hope you two have a great evening." Ariel drifted with elegance, her shoulders perfectly back and her frame straight. Cassandra gave us a smile and a wave before she left with Ariel.

I grinned as I watched them go, feeling happy for my partner and a little foolish for not noticing the obvious.

"She's cute," London noted.

"She is."

"A little too nice for Ariel, though."

I chuckled. "Ariel is a very pleasant person…when she likes you."

"Well, she needs to start liking me soon because I'm not going anywhere." London watched Ariel and Cassandra walk up to one of my biggest clients in London, a man who owned several restaurants and bars that required large shipments of scotch.

I eyed London while she was distracted, concentrating on the words she just spoke. She couldn't leave my side unless I gave her permission, but the fact that she just assumed she was going to be around for a long time gave me a strange sense of satisfaction.

My phone vibrated in my pocket, so I pulled it out and glanced at the screen.

It was Crow. *Meet me upstairs. First door on the left.*

I returned my phone to my pocket and leaned into London. "I need to attend to something. I'll be right back."

"What?" She whipped her head in my direction, horror written on her face. "Where are you going?"

"Just upstairs. I'll be back in a minute."

"I'll come with you." She grabbed my hand.

Not that I didn't enjoy her affection, but I was surprised by her neediness. "I'll be right back, Lovely. He's not even here."

"But he can show up at any moment."

"I need to talk to Crow," I whispered.

"I've been there when you've spoken to him before…"

I just didn't want people to think we snuck off together to fuck in one of the offices. But if she was this adamant about it, I wasn't going to argue with her. Besides, I liked it when she clung to me like this. She used to push me away because she despised me, and now she needed me every second around the clock.

It was a nice change.

"Okay." We walked up the stairs and reached the second landing. London kept looking around, as if she expected Crow to jump out of the shadows and scare her. I didn't understand why she was so on edge. It was like she'd never been to a party before.

I walked inside the office where Crow was waiting and shut the door behind me.

Crow was standing at the window, looking down over the entrance. With his hands in the pockets of his dark jeans, he turned around and joined us near the doorway. "Have you heard anything?"

"No." Bones said he might come by, and I didn't pressure him for a concrete answer. If I showed any special interest, it would scare him away like fish in a lake. If you wanted to survive in the underworld, you had to be on your guard constantly. Observing and studying people was the key to that. He paid attention to every word I said, every word anyone said.

Crow crossed his arms over his chest, his jaw stern with unease. He didn't look at either one of us as he contemplated his response. "Cane and my men are hiding out in the vicinity, waiting for my signal. But if she doesn't come…" Crow was difficult to read, but it was obvious that he was upset. His eyes were narrowed, and his face hadn't been shaved in days. Now it was covered with thick and coarse hair, how mine turned out if I didn't shave every day.

"We'll figure it out." Vanessa wasn't my problem and I didn't even consider Crow to be a friend, but I pitied him. I saw so much of myself in him, how devastated I was when I learned my parents and brother were never coming home. I was young at the time, but I still remembered the pain.

Crow slid his hand through his hair and glanced at the window again. "I'll keep an eye. Let me know if he contacts you."

"I will."

"And thanks for doing this. I know this isn't your problem."

I nodded. "I understand your pain. I wish I didn't, but I do."

London kept her hand in mine and gave me a gentle squeeze.

"Enjoy your party," Crow said. "Don't mind me."

I pulled London with me out of the room and to the hallway.

"I feel so bad for him," she whispered. "Do you think Bones will come?"

"I really don't know. The guy is unpredictable—which he does on purpose."

"Is there anything we can do to help?" she asked. "What if I called him…?"

I stopped and looked at her, knowing her offer was significant. She didn't even want to come tonight because she didn't want to be in the same room as him, but now she was willing to interact with him.

"What if you offered to exchange me for Vanessa? Then you could grab both of us."

The idea repulsed me. I couldn't put London in danger like that, no matter how much control I had over the situation. She was something I couldn't afford to lose, so I refused to gamble her like poker chips. "It's nice of you to offer, but I don't want you involved in this. I did the best I could. In the end, this is Crow's problem."

"This is an innocent woman we're talking about," she whispered. "It is *our* problem."

When she said things like that, it made me realize we weren't different at all. We had the same stubbornness and experienced the same heartbreak. I wanted to tear down the people who deserved it, but I never wanted to destroy an innocent person. "We have to let it go, Lovely. I did my best."

Her eyes softened when she looked at me. "I know you did…you're a good man."

Now my eyes softened. "You really think that?" I was told I was cruel and evil. This woman was my prisoner, and she said the same thing months ago. But now I felt like I was the prisoner—infatuated with this woman.

"Of course I do." Her hands slid up my chest, and she rose on her tiptoes to kiss me. Her lips were soft against my mouth, and the kiss started out subtle. It was meant to be a quick peck on the lips, but the second she felt my mouth, she remained pressed against me.

My arm tightened around her waist, and I maneuvered her against the wall, pressing her against the foundation with my hard-on right against her hip. My hand moved around her neck, and I gently felt her pulse as I kissed her, forgetting about all the people waiting for me downstairs.

Her hands moved to my shoulders, and she gave me her tongue, that sexy embrace that always made my spine shiver.

If I didn't pull away now, I'd pull her into a bedroom and fuck her. I didn't want to screw when it had to be quick and rushed. I wanted to take my time, to peel that away dress before I slid inside that wet pussy for the rest of the night.

I moved away from her and licked my lips, tasting the lipstick she wore. My thumb wiped the corner of my mouth to make sure none of the paint was on my own lips. Ordinarily, I wouldn't care. But it wasn't exactly appropriate for the black-tie event. "We'll pick this up later."

13

LONDON

I stuck to Crewe's side for the evening, doing my best to be a good conversationalist with a bunch of sophisticated strangers. My eyes kept wandering to Josephine, and every time I looked at her, she was staring at Crewe.

That pissed me off.

Crewe didn't tell me what happened between them, but based on watching their behavior, it was obvious. They were together, and he broke it off. She struggled to accept the ending of their relationship, which was why she still wanted him even though she was seeing someone else.

Whore.

She didn't even try to hide her longing. Every time I looked at her, her eyes were glued to Crewe. Her boyfriend must have noticed the same thing and didn't care. My arm was usually tucked into Crewe's arm, and I gave her a nasty glare if she stared for a little too long. When she caught my look, she quickly turned away and tried to act like she hadn't been staring in the first place.

Crewe finished his conversation before he turned back to me. "What were you doing?"

"Just looking around."

His eyes narrowed in suspicion.

"Okay, I was giving Josephine a nasty look. She won't stop staring at you."

He grinned as he enjoyed my jealousy. "Ignore her. She can stare all she wants, but it doesn't change the fact that I'm with you."

It wasn't a cheesy line, but my heart fluttered like it was.

Crewe turned to the doorway once the next guest walked inside. People were coming and going, and everywhere we turned, that was someone new to greet. "He's here."

My eyes moved to the doorway, and I spotted Bones walk inside. He wore a dark suit and blended in with the rest of the crowd. But he came alone. There wasn't a woman on his arm or anywhere in sight.

Dammit.

Crewe dropped his hand from my side. "I'm going to greet him. Stay here."

I didn't want to be anywhere near that man, but I didn't want to be vulnerable either. It would be easy for Joseph to slip one of his men inside to watch me, waiting for the perfect opportunity to grab me by the arm and point a gun into my back. My brother wasn't that aggressive, but in reality, I didn't know what he was capable of. He had been reckless enough to piss off Crewe in the first place. "No. Where you go, I go."

Crewe looked like he wanted to argue with me, but since we were in a public setting, he let it slide. "It'll be about business."

"That's fine."

"You can go mingle with Cassandra."

"No." I wasn't going anywhere.

Crewe finally dropped it, and we walked up to Bones, my arm through his. "Kind of you to drop by." They shook hands.

Bones immediately looked at me once he and Crewe had finished greeting one another. His bright blue eyes looked evil in that twisted face. I'd never forget the way he grabbed my tit like he owned me. He was disgusting, the most despicable man on the planet. I felt even more gratitude for Crewe since I was standing there with him instead of Bones. "Your date looks lovely, Crewe. Very lovely."

I moved closer into Crewe's side, feeling like bugs were crawling all over me. I didn't like it when Bones looked at me that way, like he was fucking me in his mind then and there.

Crewe circled his arm around my waist, his powerful forearm acting as a cage to keep Bones away. "Thank you. I'm a very lucky man to have this woman to myself." He hugged me tighter into his side, silently claiming me as his property.

I'd never wanted to be claimed more in my life.

Bones finally stopped staring at me, picking up on Crewe's hostility. "Quite a party."

"Too bad you didn't bring a date to enjoy it."

"She's too banged up for an appearance right now." His eyes scanned the crowd like his words had no meaning at all. Talking about beating his slave was as ordinary as a sunny day.

I wanted to stab him with a butter knife.

Crewe didn't respond to his comment. "Can I get you a drink? You know my scotch is worth your time."

"Sure," Bones answered. "You got a second to talk in private?"

"Yes." Crewe got one of the waiter's attention and motioned for him to bring them three glasses.

My heart was pounding in my chest. I knew Bones wanted to speak to Crewe in private with me nowhere in sight. But I couldn't let that happen.

Crewe handed me a glass before he nodded to the stairs. "We'll go into my office." Crewe led the way with Bones beside him.

I trailed behind, hoping neither one of them would notice until we reached the door.

We walked down the hallway until Crewe found the fifth door on the right. He opened the door and let Bones walk inside first.

I tried to pretend it was perfectly acceptable for me to be there by walking over the threshold.

"Your whore can wait downstairs," Bones said as he sat on one of the couches. He drank from his glass without looking at me.

My eyes turned to daggers, and I was about to speak my mind when Crewe grabbed me by the elbow and directed me outside. He shut the door behind him and lowered his voice. "I'll be done in five minutes, alright?"

"Crewe, I don't want to be without you." I didn't know how else to get my way unless I appealed to his ego. The more I wanted him, the more he liked it. If I really had to, I was prepared to make out with him in the hallway and rub his cock through his slacks. "I won't say anything."

"That's not the point. He doesn't want you there. I can't change his mind about that."

Shit. "I'm your woman. Where you go, I go."

His eyes darkened like he wanted to push me against the wall and fuck me right then and there. "Five minutes."

I was about to lose. "Crewe, please."

"What are you so afraid of?" he whispered.

"I'm always afraid if you aren't with me. You're the only man who makes me feel safe." It was completely out of character for me to say any of that, and I hoped Crewe didn't figure that out. Since the day we met, I always thrived alone. I didn't need anyone to take care of me. I'd been looking after myself for a long time. But the more I wanted him, the more powerful it made him feel. There was nothing Crewe wanted more than power.

Crewe's annoyance dimmed slightly. "You can stay in the hallway if you want. But we need to have this conversation in private."

I knew that was his final answer and arguing wouldn't make any difference.

He grabbed my chin with his fingertips and pressed a kiss to my lips. It was tender and soft, a quiet apology since I couldn't get what I wanted. He walked inside and shut the door behind him. The last thing I heard was him speaking to Bones. "Call her a whore again, and I'll kill you."

Bones chuckled. "Ah, so she's not your whore. Can't blame you. She really is beautiful."

Their voices trailed away, and I couldn't hear their words anymore. I stayed in the hallway and looked from left to right. Crow was in the first room near the staircase, and I considered joining him. But I knew Crewe would be pissed that I'd crossed the line with his client. I shouldn't interfere when I didn't have anything to do with the drama unfolding at this party.

I considered going back downstairs and joining the party. If I stuck to Ariel's side, I'd probably be fine. She was observant, so it would be stupid for Joseph or one of his men to make a move. But I might also be putting myself in the spotlight. If they watched me walk away with Crewe, they probably assumed we were still together.

Nothing had happened so far, so I decided to stay put.

Fifteen minutes later, I heard a door click far down the hallway. The lights were on, but the pathway was dimly lit. I searched for someone to appear out of the doorway, but there was no movement.

I got a bad feeling in the pit of my stomach.

I heard the noise again, and that's when I spotted Joseph emerge from one of the doorways. One of his men was behind him, carrying an AK-47.

"Jesus…"

I grabbed the door and twisted the knob, but of course, it was locked. "Crewe?" I banged my fist on the door.

I didn't get a response.

I turned to Joseph again, who was walking quicker now. He wanted to snatch me and run. I shook my head vigorously and waved my hand in front of my face, telling him to turn back.

Joseph shook his head in response.

"Crewe?" I knocked again.

Thankfully, the door flew open, and Crewe emerged. "You're lucky we're finished because we don't appreciate your impatience."

Joseph was still coming down the hallway, but he halted when Crewe emerged.

If I didn't do something, Crewe would see him. And if Crewe saw him, Joseph's men would fire. Bones was probably packing, so he would shoot Joseph. No good would come from any of it.

I cupped Crewe's face and kissed him as I backed him back into the room, moving my mouth hard with his so he would be knocked off-balance. I pressed my body into his and circled my arms around his neck, giving him everything I had so he wouldn't step into that hallway. Bones was probably watching the whole thing, but that wasn't important right now.

Crewe eventually broke away, and judging from the look on his face, he wasn't annoyed with the affection. He just wanted more of it.

"No wonder why you didn't let this one go." Bones walked around us and entered the hallway. "Let me know what you think about our arrangement, Crewe." He disappeared, leaving us alone.

I suspected Joseph had taken off. If there were a man in the hallway carrying a huge gun, Bones would have said something.

Crisis averted.

Crewe pressed his hand against the door and pushed it closed. The second we were alone together, I knew exactly what was coming next. His hands moved to his belt and the button at the top of his slacks. His pants came loose, and he pushed them to his ankles. "I wanted to wait until the evening was over, but you aren't giving me much of a choice." He turned me around and pushed me hard against the wall and hiked my dress around my waist. My thong was pulled past my thighs, and he shoved himself harshly inside me.

I gripped the wall for balance as I felt him pound into me. I was glad my clinginess had led to sex as opposed to a fight, and I was even more grateful I kept Joseph and Crewe away from one another.

Otherwise, they'd both be dead.

14

LONDON

Now that I was back at the castle, life returned to normal. I sat outside in the courtyard and read while Crewe worked all day. It took me some time to get over the opening, the fact that Josephine was a beautiful duchess who still wanted Crewe, Crow didn't get his sister back, Bones was still vile, and Joseph had stupidly risked his neck to get me out of there.

The castle never felt so comfortable.

I wanted to stay behind these walls forever and enjoy the peace of being hidden away. Joseph couldn't get me when I was surrounded by walls of solid stone. He certainly couldn't get me while all of Crewe's men watched the property constantly.

I could finally relax.

Crewe stepped into the garden in his black suit and tie. It'd become a pattern for us to spend lunch together. With every passing week, we fell into a deeper routine mixed with meals, sex, and working out.

He wore his aviator sunglasses, looking like a man on vacation more than one at work. When he reached my chair, his hands gripped each of the armrests, and he leaned down to kiss me. He didn't give me much time to prepare, and that was clearly on purpose. He gave me a hard kiss on the mouth before he sat in the chair next to me. The maids had brought me a pot of tea and some milk. I didn't care for tea before I came here, but it grew on me after a few months. "Enjoying your day?"

"Yeah." I closed the book and set it on the table. "I went for a run then lifted some weights. Then I showered and headed down here. It's nice to get some sun." Since I didn't get out in any other way.

"I thought you looked sexier than usual." He wore a smug smile that was supposed to be arrogant, but of course, it was sexy on him. Everything he did was sexy, even though I would never admit it to his face.

"Nope. Flabby as usual."

"You're not flabby," he said with a chuckle. "You're perfect in every way possible."

The warmth spread throughout my body when I heard the compliment. The fact that he was sincere made me feel special. He said the sweetest things when I least expected it. He was romantic and affectionate, completely opposite of when we first met. "Maybe you think being flabby is perfect."

"I think being you is perfect." He grabbed my cup of tea and took a drink.

"You should be a diplomat."

"I always know the right things to say, huh?" He poured more hot tea into the cup and added a drop of honey before he leaned back and sipped it.

I hardly saw him drink scotch anymore, and his mood was noticeably lighter. I knew he didn't quit cold turkey, but at least now he was drinking a reasonable amount. He seemed happier too, but maybe that was because of different reasons. "Get a lot of work done today?"

"There's not enough hours in the day, even with Ariel working twice as many hours as I do."

"I'd offer to help, but I doubt I could be useful."

"Even if you were, I'd rather you sit back and relax."

And I'd rather be finishing my education so I could do something productive with my life, not sit around and get fat. "How's Crow?"

He stirred the tea before he set the spoon on the saucer. He was a grown man with enormous hands, so it was comical to see him drink out of a small teacup like a woman at breakfast. "He's alright." His mood darkened when I mentioned his client. "I wish Bones had brought Vanessa. It's a shame he didn't."

"I feel so bad for Crow."

"I'm sure he'll find a way. When it comes to family, you never stop."

I hoped for her sake Crow and Cane would figure out a way to save her. No woman should be subjected to that monster. I didn't like it when he even looked at me. Being touched by him would be pure torture. "Yeah…"

He took another sip of the tea before he handed it back to me. "Have you ever tried it with honey?"

"I can't say I have."

"Give it a go."

I took a sip and enjoyed the smooth sweetness as it moved across my tongue. "Not bad."

"That's how my mother used to drink it."

"Oh…" I was surprised he remembered something like that.

He watched me from his seat, his eyes a mystery since they were hidden behind his sunglasses. I didn't like it when anything was obstructing his face because it was difficult to figure out what he was thinking.

I leaned forward and slowly pulled the sunglasses off the bridge of his nose and set them on the table. "There. That's better."

"Yeah?"

"Yeah." I moved over the table with my elbows resting on the surface and pressed a gentle kiss to his mouth. "I can see your eyes. And your eyes are my favorite." I pulled away, seeing his heavy-lidded expression.

A slight smile moved across his mouth, and his eyes narrowed intently on my face. He stared at me with that focused expression, making me feel like the only thing that mattered in this world. It was a look that made me both hot and cold at the same time. "Why?"

"Because I can see your mood, your thoughts."

"You can read my mind?" he whispered.

"Not your mind. Just your emotions."

"Then what am I feeling now?"

That was easy. "That you want to keep kissing me. Just kiss me. You don't want to take it to the bedroom where the clothes will come off. You want to feel our mouths move together, our tongues slide past one another. You want my hands to move up and down your chest while you fist my hair. And you want to keep doing that…until it's time for you to leave." I wasn't sure if that was exactly what was on his mind, but it was on mine. I could tell when he was in a purely sexual mood, and that wasn't now. But he was definitely affectionate, definitely warm.

His eyes narrowed even more, and the smile left his face. "Maybe you can read my mind."

"Your eyes give you away."

"Then maybe I should put those sunglasses back on."

"No." I pulled them farther away from his grasp so I could see all of his handsome face. "I want to look at you. It's much nicer than the view."

He leaned back into his chair and watched me, his eyes darkening in a way I'd never seen before. He didn't say another word, and his playfulness disappeared. The silence stretched between us, but it wasn't uncomfortable. It was heavy with unspoken words, scorching attraction, and everything else that existed between us.

I couldn't read his mood like I usually could because his thoughts were different from what they ever were before. Something changed. I could feel it in the air as well as see it in his eyes. I just wasn't sure what that change was.

I hoped I would find out.

I jogged around the castle because there were dirt pathways that maneuvered through the grass and the trees. His guards were around the property everywhere, so I never felt unsupervised. All of the men had obviously been told I had permission to go wherever I wanted because they never tried to stop me.

I pulled the earbuds out of my ears and slowed to a walk. I had a stitch in my side, and I struggled to relax the muscle around my waist. My hands moved to my hips, and I breathed through my nose and out my mouth. I knew Crewe took this path every single day, but he went at the crack of dawn when I was still asleep.

I couldn't get up early even to eat, let alone work out.

I nearly jumped out of my skin when Dunbar emerged on the path, wearing black jeans and a black t-shirt. I was suddenly aware of how alone we were together. None of the other guards was anywhere nearby. Crewe would never hear my screams no matter how loud I yelled.

So I'd have to kill Dunbar.

I had an iPod in my hand, and I could crush it against his nose if I had to.

Dunbar looked like he wanted to strangle me, crack my neck like I was a chicken on the farm. He stopped in his tracks ten feet away and didn't come any closer.

I watched him, my hand gripping the music device. "Yes?"

"I'm going to tell you something. But you didn't hear it from me. Accuse me, and I'll deny it."

I raised an eyebrow, having no idea where this was going. "Okay…"

"The device that Crewe put inside your brother's head… it's not real." His bushy eyebrows moved every time he spoke, his expression concentrated on the severity of the moment.

"What?"

"It's not wired to an electric pulse. It just carries a signal so it'll show up on an X-ray."

My hands gripped my waist as I listened to every word. "Why would Crewe do that?"

"Because Crewe wouldn't want to kill your brother. He just wants you to think he will."

"Because…?"

"It keeps both of you in line."

Come to think of it, I never saw Crewe with the transmitter on him. He never threatened me with the explosive either. "If that's true, why would you tell me?"

"Isn't it obvious?" he hissed. "Ever since you came around, you've been sabotaging my every move—"

"Have not."

"Yes, you have. Crewe is so obsessed with you that he's losing his focus. I know you've been manipulating him this entire time. Ariel agrees with me. You're going to pull him down a path he can't recover from. But now that you know the truth, you can leave. Find an escape route and go."

Dunbar wasn't trustworthy so I didn't know if I could believe a word he said, but I did believe his motives. He'd wanted me out of here since the day I arrived. He had no problem strangling me and slapping me. Both he and Ariel wanted me out of Crewe's life. And this was the perfect way to get rid of me. "How do I know you aren't lying? That you're just trying to get my brother and me dead?"

"I don't care about either of you being dead. I just want you gone. You wanna know how I'm telling the truth? Think about Crewe. He's a hard man, but he's not cruel. He didn't sell you to Bones because he went soft. He hasn't hurt you because he's kind. He defended you from me because he's chivalrous. Do you really think he would hurt you, the woman his entire universe revolves around?"

When he said that, there wasn't a doubt in my mind.

Dunbar was telling the truth.

There wasn't a bomb inside my brother's head.

There was nothing keeping me there.

All I had to do was plan my next move.

And I could be free.

15

CREWE

Ariel sat with her leather notepad on her lap. A glass of scotch was on the table beside her, and she was on her second drink. Pias sat in the other chair, our main distributor who took care of the shipments before they headed off to international places. He was essential in my scotch business, and he was someone Ariel approved of.

One of the butlers came to my side and lifted the decanter of scotch. "Another, sir?"

I eyed the empty glass and didn't struggle to resist. "I'd prefer a glass of water. Thank you."

"Very well, sir." He grabbed the pitcher and filled my glass.

Ariel lifted her gaze from her notebook and looked at me. It was obvious what she was thinking. She didn't need to say it.

Pias gave us a report about the recent shipment to the Middle East. He was one of the foot soldiers that was responsible for packaging our quality product and ensuring it reached our clients in the perfect condition. That wasn't something a factory of robots could do.

Ariel scribbled her notes. "I'm glad everything is going smoothly. Sales have spiked since the opening."

I rested my fingertips against my lips. "No surprise there." All of the nobility got to sample my scotch firsthand. It was a nice respite from all the French wines they drank on a daily basis. Scotch wasn't just a man's drink—it was everyone's drink.

Ariel stared at me with narrowed eyes, her passive-aggressive attitude leaking from her pores. She was waiting for me to ask what her problem was.

But I wasn't gonna take the bait.

Dimitri opened the door to the drawing room then came to my side. He leaned down to my ear and whispered his message. "Lady London is asking for you. Should I tell her you're in a meeting?"

The second she was on my mind, I didn't want to think about anything else. I wanted to circle my arms around her waist and kiss her, even if it was only for a few minutes. Then I would return to this dry meeting so Ariel could continue to shoot me glares. "I'll see her." I rose from my chair. "Excuse me. Carry on without me."

Ariel looked like she wanted to kill me. "You can't expect us to carry on when you're the owner of this fine business." She gripped her black pen until her knuckles turned white. With those black glasses on the bridge of her nose, she looked even more terse.

I didn't care for her attitude. "That's a good point, Ariel."

She relaxed, like she assumed her words got to me.

"You can wait until I'm ready to return."

Now she really wanted to rip her claws into me.

I walked out without looking back, knowing her anger would have tripled by the time I returned. I closed the thick door behind me and saw London standing near the staircase in pastel blue dress and nude heels. Dimitri arranged for her clothing to be put into the closet, and everything looked spectacular on her. She had the perfect figure, so everything fit nicely. She hadn't noticed me yet, so I took advantage of the next few seconds to appreciate the sight of her.

She really was the most beautiful woman I'd ever seen.

And she was mine.

I walked toward her with my hands in my pockets, playing it cool even though my heart was racing in my chest. She made my body tense and excited in a way no one else ever had. I was used to sharing my life with her, but now there was this indescribable electricity between us. I could feel it anytime I was near her.

When her eyes landed on me, they widened imperceptibly, but I paid enough attention to notice the small detail. She looked just as pleased to see me even though I'd only been gone for a few hours.

"Yes?" My arms circled her petite waistline, and I positioned her perfectly against my chest, my lips moving to hers in a sensual embrace. My mouth hesitated the second I touched hers, feeling that energy I'd become reliant on. I moved my hand into her hair, and I pulled her tighter against me as the kiss quickened on its own. I took several steps forward and guided her against the wall, getting her in a perfect spot she couldn't slip away from —not that she would try.

Her hands started at my waistline where she fingered the loops on my pants. She gave a quick tug and pulled me tighter against her, wanting more of me even though I'd already given her everything. Her hands moved to my waist next then slowly slid up my chest until she felt my shoulders. I knew how much she loved my body because she touched me the exact same way every morning and every night.

The kiss went on for minutes, and while I was hard in my slacks, I didn't think about taking her upstairs into our bedroom. I was content with this kiss, with this embrace that made my entire body come alive. I'd never kissed a woman like I did with her. Her mouth was enough for me. I was satisfied with so little even though I usually craved so much more. It didn't make any sense.

I finally pulled away when ten minutes passed, knowing I couldn't keep Ariel and Pias waiting forever. My hands remained on her tiny waistline, the perfect position to get a tight grip on her. My face pressed against hers, and I stared at her lips, not really thinking about anything. It was the only sense of Zen I ever received, the existence of absolute peace. She somehow bestowed it on me. "Did you need something?"

Her hands remained against my chest, and her words came out as a whisper. "Wanted to see if you wanted to have lunch together…"

"I'm having a meeting right now, but we'll be finished soon."

"Okay. I'll see you then." She kissed the corner of my mouth, her lips moving over the thick hair that had come in since I skipped the shave that morning. "Sorry that I interrupted you."

"You never interrupt me." My hands cupped her face, and I gave her another kiss, needing something to hold me over until I was finished speaking with Ariel and Pias. I forced myself to step away before I kissed her hard all over again. Then another ten minutes would pass, and Ariel would only be angrier.

I walked back inside and felt the tension the second I entered the room. I knew shit was about to hit the fan because Pias was nowhere in sight. Ariel had obviously excused him so she could speak to me in private.

I knew it was coming.

"Crewe, I'm very concerned about you and that woman."

"I can tell." I drank my water to mask my irritation. I didn't tell Ariel off like I normally would with someone else. She was a great business partner and deserved more respect than that. I wasn't ignorant of her capabilities. But if she pushed me too far, I would come undone.

"I'm serious. You said she didn't mean anything to you, but I see the way you look at her."

"And have you seen the way she looks at me?" London couldn't get enough of me. Every morning when I left the sheets, she begged me to stay with her. During our meals together, her hands were usually on my body—her eyes glued to mine. When we fucked at night, she was all over me. She took my cock like she wanted it as much as I gave it to her, and when we slept, she was wrapped around me like a child with a teddy bear. I wasn't stupid.

I knew she loved me.

I didn't know when it happened, exactly. But at that opening, she was fiercely jealous of Josephine—not that there was anything to be jealous of. She didn't want to leave my side—not even for a second. I was the center of her universe. She was pissed that she'd been taken from her home, but now she didn't care anymore.

I was home.

The realization didn't bother me. I loved her infatuation, her obsession. I loved it when she demanded that I be faithful to her. Her need only made me need her more. I'd never been turned on by clinginess or commitment, but I liked knowing London needed me.

That she wanted me.

Ariel shut her notebook, her lips pursed and her eyes angry. "Crewe, you gave me your word that this meant nothing. You told me you would marry a suitable partner."

"Who said anything about getting married?"

"Well, it doesn't look like you've made any progress on finding a partner—unless you've chosen her."

I drank my water again and considered pouring myself a glass of scotch. I'd been sticking to my new diet, but this interrogation made me want to slip. "Ariel, I don't stick my nose in your business. Don't stick your nose in mine. Who I fuck is none of your concern."

"I don't give a damn who you fuck. I give a damn who you love. Crewe, she's not right for you."

"I never said I loved her."

"Are you saying you don't?"

I stared her down.

She sighed and pulled her glasses off. "That woman is smart. She's manipulating you, Crewe."

"Manipulating me how?"

"She thinks you have a bomb in her brother's head. Of course she's playing nice so you remove it."

I shook my head. "No one is that good of an actress. Her feelings are genuine."

She rolled her eyes. "Come on, Crewe. I see right through her little act. It's all a game."

Ariel didn't fuck her every night. "Let me handle my sex life. Worry about your own."

"I don't give a damn about your sex life. It's repulsive, honestly. But who you marry directly affects my involvement in your business. You already know this, Crewe."

"Like I said, I'm not getting married."

"But you're definitely on the path to a poor choice," she hissed.

"Don't worry about our business. We're up by fifty percent since last year. We're growing."

"And we'll plateau if we don't keep working. The second you get comfortable, that's when things go to shit."

"I've been doing this for a long time, Ariel. You need to calm down."

She looked like she might throw her glass of scotch in my face. "You have other avenues of wealth, an inheritance that most countries can't even afford. I'm not so fortunate, Crewe. This is all I have. I'm not willing to gamble it."

"I would never let that happen, Ariel. Our wealth will always be secure. The business will maintain itself even if I never get married at all."

"But it'll never grow unless you marry someone like Princess Leonida of Russia."

I nearly crushed the glass in my hand. "You know I'd never marry someone like her." I'd never have any ties to

Russia as long as I lived. They were my enemy, as far as I was concerned.

"But you understand what I'm saying, Crewe. It can't be some medical school dropout from Brooklyn."

I'd already said this twice. "Again, marriage isn't on my mind, Ariel."

"For now," she said coldly. "This woman is going to make a mockery out of you. You're smarter than this. She's distracting you from what's important. She's manipulating you, and you don't even realize it."

I couldn't disagree more. "Ariel, enough."

"No. She's—"

I held up my hand. "*Enough.*"

Ariel shut her mouth, but her eyes burned like she had more to say.

"You've made your feelings perfectly clear. I don't need to hear you repeat them fifteen more times." I rose from the chair, my hand shaking with the urge to hit something. "Focus on your job. That's what I'm paying you to do."

I retreated into my office, the one place in the world that was solely mine. I owned lots of real estate, but I had to share that space with dozens of employees. My bedroom was occupied by London, who was probably waiting for me to tell her I was ready for lunch.

I chose to hide out in here instead.

There was a light knock on the door before London stepped inside. She took one look at me and immediately knew something was wrong because she shut the door and walked inside without being invited. She walked to my desk then took a seat on the edge, crossing her legs and facing the large window behind me.

I didn't look at her, my ankle resting on the opposite knee and my fingertips against my lips. I swayed slightly from left to right, replaying my conversation was Ariel over and over. I understood she had a personal interest in her investment, but she was blowing this out of proportion.

"Anything I can do?" London knew me well enough that she understood not to ask me what happened. When she pushed for details, it just pushed me away instead.

"No."

She looked out the window and pulled her hair over one shoulder. Even out of the corner of my eye, she looked beautiful. It was hard not to believe we'd just kissed so passionately thirty minutes ago. "You want me to leave you alone?"

Any other time, I would have immediately answered yes. But I didn't want her to go anywhere. Her presence sheathed my anger. Her beauty made me feel calm. I straightened my legs then patted my thigh. "No."

A slight expression of surprise came over her face before she straddled my hips. Her dress rose up her thighs when she spread her legs, and her arms wrapped around my shoulders.

My hands moved to her hips, and I stared at her without saying a word. Direct eye contact was usually an act of hostility, but looking into her eyes made my irritation wash away. I could hold the intimate look and feel better, not worse. I didn't care if she could read my emotions because I had nothing to hide—not from her. "I got into a fight with Ariel." London hadn't asked me anything, but the words came out anyway. I didn't see her as a woman who was in my captivity anymore. She wasn't just some woman I was sleeping with. I saw her as something much more than that—saw her as a friend.

My closest friend.

She watched me in silence, never asking for more than what I gave.

"She thinks you're a distraction."

"Well…she's not totally wrong. I interrupt you when you're working all the time." Her hands slid down my chest, and she watched her own movements. "I won't do it anymore."

I loved it when she interrupted me. I lived for those moments. When she slipped me a note and invited me upstairs to fuck her, I was harder than a rock. "No. I look forward to those interruptions."

"Maybe I'll take a break for a while…get on Ariel's good side."

She could never get on her good side.

"I can try talking to her. I don't want to make your life more stressful."

I already knew how that conversation would go. "That wouldn't do any good. She doesn't trust you, thinks you're manipulating me." I didn't accuse London of anything because I didn't suspect her in any regard. I knew Ariel was wrong, so I didn't need to question London about it.

London stared at me, her eyes unblinking. "Manipulating you…?"

"Trying to soften me to get your way. I told her to knock it off. I'm sick of listening to her paranoia." I didn't mention the part about marriage. London and I hadn't had a conversation about our future or where our relationship stood, and I wasn't excited to have one either.

Her hands slid down my chest to my stomach, where her fingertips gently pressed against my collared shirt. Her eyes were downcast, and she was quiet.

I knew how she felt about me, so this conversation was probably offensive. But I made it clear I didn't share Ariel's beliefs. "The only reason why I put up with Ariel is because she's good at what she does. The best, actually. She's entitled to her opinion, of course. I just get sick of listening to her criticize my sex life."

"She's just looking out for you."

I raised an eyebrow, surprised London would defend her.

"That's also her job, being honest with you even though it'll make you angry. I know it's annoying, but she's loyal

328 | PENELOPE SKY

to you. Any criticism she gives comes from a good place. She has your back, Crewe."

I stared at her in surprise, unable to believe that London could say something good about Ariel when Ariel had nothing but mean things to say about her. That only convinced me that Ariel was being overly paranoid. "Hungry?"

"You know the answer."

I rose to my feet and lifted her with me, her body light as a feather. A simple conversation with her had completely flipped my mood. She was the only person capable of making the impossible happen.

I held her against my chest with her legs wrapped around my waist. My hand gripped her ass, feeling the smooth skin underneath her dress. I had an appetite just a moment ago, but now I was in the mood for something else.

Her eyes darkened like she could read my mind.

I laid her down on my desk, aroused by the stark contrast between her fair skin and the dark mahogany wood. I'd never taken any other woman in my office besides London. She was the only one to have the pleasure of infecting my entire life.

I pulled her panties off and hiked up her dress to her waist. My slacks and boxers fell to my ankles, and I positioned her ass slightly off the desk. My cock was already twitching, and I knew her pussy was wet without even checking. I shoved my dick inside her roughly, wanting to claim her as soon as possible. My eyes honed in on her reaction, watching her cheeks flush and her breathing hitch.

She gripped my wrists as I held on to her thighs. Her nails dug into my skin the harder I gripped her, and nearly silent moans escaped her lips before I even moved.

This was not just an act.

This was all real.

I knew it.

16

LONDON

Ariel wasn't stupid.

She was onto me.

An intelligent woman liked that noticed everything under her nose. She knew Crewe better than I did, so she knew when his behavior was out of the ordinary. She knew he was changing just the way I noticed he was changing.

But that meant my plan was working.

Crewe didn't share Ariel's suspicions at all.

He trusted me.

That actually made me feel terrible. Guilt overwhelmed me when it shouldn't, and I found myself questioning the plan I'd set out. But I had to remind myself that I was a prisoner when I should be a free woman. Even if my anger had softened, that didn't change my circumstances.

I deserved to be free.

I had to keep moving forward. Once Crewe gave me a clear sign that what we had was real, I'd finally have the courage to ask him if I could leave. I could plan another escape since the guards weren't as suspicious anymore, but that would probably backfire. And I felt like Crewe deserved more than a breakout in the middle of the night.

If he had a heart like I thought he did, we could come to an understanding. He would let me go because he knew it was the right thing to do. Our relationship had changed so much, and we couldn't stay this way any longer.

He cared about me.

He respected me.

He would let me go.

I knew he would.

A week went by, and Crewe was back to being in a good mood. Ariel must have dropped her argument, and they returned to their comfortable business relationship, focusing on numbers and scotch. We shared all our meals together and had amazing sex at night. It was as good as it was going to get.

Fall had set in, so it was a cool day. The sky was overcast with heavy clouds that hinted at rain, so I stayed in the royal chambers in the private living room while the fire roared in the hearth. There was a nice collection of books on the shelf, so I made my way through each one. Some of them were first editions, Scottish literature that would be worth thousands if they were taken to market. They were special antiques that filled the air with dust and time, making me feel like I was in a different century.

Crewe finished working after five and walked inside, stripping his jacket and tie by the door. "Lovely?" He called out to me when he couldn't see me in the bedroom.

I suddenly felt like a married couple, the husband coming home and announcing his presence to his wife.

I liked it and hated it. "I'm in here."

Crewe walked in as he unbuttoned his white collared shirt. He didn't smile when he stood near the couch and looked at me. He stared at me with an expression I'd become used to. It was nothing but intensity, the way he showed he was excited to see me.

My heart still fluttered just as it did the first time he did it. I wished it wouldn't, but I couldn't control all the impulses my body made. I shut the book and rested it on my lap. "Get a lot of work done today?"

"Some." His shirt was open, showing his perfectly chiseled physique. "Not as much as I would like."

"Maybe you need to hire another Ariel."

"I would if such a person existed." He stripped off his shirt and tossed it on the armrest of the couch.

I tried not to stare at his glorious body, but that was nearly impossible to do. He was the sexiest man I knew for a reason. He was all muscle and skin, not an inch of fat anywhere. He had nice, toned arms, his muscles defined and powerful. I liked seeing him undress the second he came into the bedroom. He usually stripped down to his boxers and sometimes threw sweat pants on. I didn't even realize I was biting my bottom lip until the light pressure became uncomfortable.

He slid his belt out of the loops then folded it in half. When he yanked on both sides, the leather smacked together and made a noticeable crack.

He hadn't spanked me in a long time. Kinda missed it.

His pants and shoes came next before he sat beside me on the couch, glorious in just his boxers. His arm rested over the back of the couch, and he stared at the fire as the sun disappeared from the windows. It was nearly dark.

His hand moved to the back of my head, and he gently touched my hair, what he usually did when he was sitting beside me.

I felt the bumps sprinkle across my arms. I didn't know if I was nervous about the fact that I was playing him or if it was because I actually felt something. The intensity of the emotions made it impossible to differentiate.

When I felt his gaze on me, my mouth went dry. My thighs automatically squeezed together, and I forgot about the book I was reading altogether. Couldn't even remember what it was called.

His hand slowly turned my head so I would look him in the eye. His fingers dug into my hair as well as my scalp, exerting silent control over me without any resistance.

I met his look, seeing the bright irises surrounding the center of his eyes that were highlighted from the flames. I'd never cared for brown eyes, always preferring men with green or blue irises, but his were the prettiest I'd ever seen. They were the same color as the scotch he drank, and they suited him perfectly. The color was tuned to his dark mood, which sometimes lightened if he was having a good day.

I swallowed the lump in my throat, my mouth dry. My nerves lit on fire, my fingertips burning as well as everything else. My thighs squeezed harder when the interaction began to feel like it was the first time we'd ever touched.

It was definitely the first time we ever touched like this.

He was different. I was different.

Everything was different.

His fingers fisted my hair, getting a tight grip before he leaned in and kissed me. It was a simple kiss without tongue, but it still took my breath away. His lips hardly moved with mine, and all the passion was felt in his restraint rather than his movements.

He pulled away and looked at me, but I knew that wasn't the end of it. That was just a slow beginning—a slow burn that would turn into a roaring fire.

I yanked down the front of his boxers so his cock could come free. When I went down on him, his pleasure was always the biggest thing on my mind. I wanted to make him feel good, to make him come back to me instead of looking for sex elsewhere. But now I didn't think about his pleasure or how this could forward my agenda.

I just wanted him in my mouth.

I leaned over and licked the head of his enormous cock, my ass in the air. His hand moved up my thigh and yanked my dress up so he could rub his hand over my ass. My hand wrapped around his impressive girth, and I slid most of his length inside my mouth, ignoring the uncomfortable stretching of my throat and just enjoying the way he tasted.

I loved the way he tasted.

His hand kept the hair out of my face, and he watched me with a stern jaw and a hard expression. His eyes followed every move I made, the arousal heavy in his eyes. When his breathing changed, I could hear it. Louder and louder it became as he enjoyed my wet mouth surrounding him.

I sucked the juice from his tip then pushed him as far back as my throat could handle, feeling my gag reflex struggle not to go off. I kept going because I wanted him, all of him.

"Fuck..." His hand moved to the back of my neck, and he guided me up and down his length, moving slowly as he wanted to enjoy every steady thrust as he slid into my mouth. Saliva dripped down his length and to his balls, and I moved my mouth to his sac so I could suck it back into my mouth and return it to his length.

His fingers dug into me harder.

I wanted to keep going, but I also wanted that big cock inside me. We were both so wet and anxious for each other, and I could hardly stop my legs from shaking. I wanted him every morning and every night, but I particularly wanted him now.

I pulled my mouth away, a sticky line of saliva forming between my mouth and his tip. I wiped it away with my fingers as I sat up, feeling that scorching gaze practically burn a hole right through my skin.

Crewe immediately moved me to my back and nearly ripped the dress off me. He treated the zipper with violence, nearly breaking it as he dragged it to the top of my ass. Once my straps were loose, he peeled them down my arms until he could get it off with one swift tug. When we were in his office, the only thing he removed was my underwear. But when we had no interruptions, he wanted me in nothing but skin.

I pushed his boxers down to his ankles, and he kicked them away, making him beautiful and naked on top of me.

He wrapped one leg around my waist and pinned me into the couch, my head resting on the armrest. The fire was still burning, acting as the only light in the living room. The sun was gone now, and all we could hear was the flicker of the flames. One of the maids would announce dinner, but neither one of us would hear the door.

My hands snaked up his powerful chest and to the back of his neck, my pussy begging to feel his cock inside me. I breathed against his mouth, anxious for him to fill me with every inch of his length.

He purposely dragged it out, teasing me on purpose. He brushed his lips past mine and rubbed his length against my folds. I was soaked and so was he, so we slipped past one another without resistant. When he rubbed against my clit, my bottom lip quivered.

My nails dug into his shoulders. "Crewe, make love to me." I looked him in the eye as I whispered my request, knowing he would grant it. It wasn't like him to make me beg for too long. He didn't have the restraint.

He pointed his length inside me and slid through my wet tightness, a masculine moan accompanying his movements. His arms tightened as he suspended himself above me, the scruff of his face brushing against my cheek.

My nails cut into his skin deeply, and I let out a moan that rivaled his. My eyes closed for a moment as the shiver of excitement ran up my spine. The fire burned and crackled in the background, but the sound of his breathing was in the forefront. Everything outside of that room didn't exist. It was just the two of us in the middle of nowhere, making love in a stone castle built by his ancestors. I wanted him for more reasons than just to get off. I wanted him because I missed him all day. I missed him the second he left for work in the morning.

I missed my captor.

He rocked into me slowly, his long length stretching me over and over every time he moved. Every time his powerful body moved, his muscles rippled and shifted under the skin. He was a mass of power and strength, and he was stronger than the stone walls that surrounded the castle.

My hands kissed his body as they trailed down his back, feeling the muscles shift under my touch. My fingers had a mind of their own, and I dug into him harder than I meant to, gripping his body like it was grooves on a mountainside.

Crewe positioned my other leg against his chest and deepened the angle, giving me his entire length as he moved inside me. His breathing accelerated as his hips thrust harder. When sweat formed on his skin, the drops reflected the firelight.

"Crewe…" My fingers dove into his hair, and I felt the sweat coat my fingertips. I was already on the verge of exploding, but my quickness to come was no longer surprising. This man made me crumble so easily because he knew my body better than I did. He knew exactly where all my buttons were and how to set them off.

He kissed me hard as he continued his pace, fucking me with long and even strokes. His cock hit me in the perfect location every single time, lighting me on fire as if he'd just drenched me with gasoline.

His tongue dove into my mouth and met mine with enthusiasm, swirling together in a heated embrace. I could kiss him a million times and never get tired of it. Every touch was just as good as the first one. His hands made my curves feel more feminine. His kiss made me feel more beautiful. And his heart made me feel safer than anywhere else in the world.

I wrapped my arms around his neck and looked him in the eye, seeing his intensity match mine. I'd never had this kind of passion with another man. I'd never shown it or been the recipient either. It was the kind that made my toes curl and my moans turn to pants. "Crewe…I love you."

His pace slowed instantly, his strokes becoming longer and more spaced out, but he never stopped. He held my gaze with a hard expression, his emotions tucked away on purpose so I couldn't see them.

I wasn't thinking when I blurted those words out. I knew I needed to get him wrapped around my finger if I ever had any hope of leaving this place. Maybe my subconscious was doing the fighting for me, making sure I got out of there as quickly as possible.

If he didn't say it back, it was just going to halt all the progress I'd made. It would make things awkward between us, ruining the beautiful companionship we'd grown from nothing. My hands dragged down his shoulders, and I rocked my hips to take his length again. I kept my eyes glued to his, hoping I would get something out of him. If I didn't, at least I didn't want to chase him away.

But the damage was done.

To mask the tension, I pulled his lips to mine and kissed him again, my lower body working to take his length with the same excitement he showed earlier. I was still about to come, and once we got back up to speed, I would have my explosion.

Crewe thrust his hips hard again, fucking me with the intensity as he did before. His lips moved against mine until he lost his concentration, feeling so many things at once. I couldn't kiss him anymore either because all I could do was breathe. I knew the combustion was coming, the sizzling heat that was going to ignite me in an inferno so hot that I would melt to the touch.

After a few more thrusts of his cock, I felt the explosion begin at my core and reach everywhere else. The sensation burned from my fingertips to my toes, making me pant and moan incoherently. The pleasure was so profound I couldn't make out a single word other than a scream. My arms locked around his body as I rode the high as long as possible. The tenderness started between my legs and moved all the way up to my belly. All I felt was pure pleasure, even when the orgasm passed. I existed in a pleasure coma, existing only to feel.

Crewe's eyes remained on me the entire time, watching my over-the-top performance. He moved his mouth to mine and kissed me again. "I love you, Lovely." He spoke against my lips, his eyes heavy-lidded but open. He brushed his nose against mine before he kissed me again, his cock continuing to pierce me with impressive thrusts.

I felt something I couldn't describe, and I couldn't describe it because I'd never felt it before. It was a form of joy, higher than unbridled happiness that made me feel a spectrum of colors in my chest. My hands tightened their grip, and I felt my pussy clench around his cock for an entirely different reason. Waves of heat pierced my body everywhere, lifting me to a new state of being.

I looked into his eyes and pressed my hands against his chest. I could feel every time he breathed, every time his muscles flexed as he moved. I moved my right hand over his heart, feeling his pulse work at full speed to please me.

Crewe pressed his forehead to mine and gave his final pumps. His breathing deepened as he reached the end of his restraint. He released a quiet grunt before he shoved himself completely inside me, giving me all of his come.

I grabbed his ass and tugged him harder even though there was no room left. I just wanted every drop of his seed, every ounce of his arousal.

His eyes darkened at my actions, and he sucked my bottom lip into his mouth, moaning as he felt me.

My tongue entered his mouth, and I continued to pull him hard into me, not wanting his cock to go anywhere even though it was softening. I wanted him to stay buried inside me until he was hard and ready to go again. "Give me more."

He kissed my neck and my jawline. "Want more of my come, Lovely?"

"I want it all."

We lay on the rug in front of the fireplace wrapped up in a blanket Crewe had pulled off the couch. He threw another log onto the fire when the flames burned too low, and we were warmed by the heat that filled the room. After several rounds of sex, we were too tired to do anything besides lie together.

Crewe held me against his body while he kept his eyes closed. He wasn't asleep, but he didn't have as much energy as he usually did—because he used it all up on me. Somehow, he looked even more handsome when he was relaxed. His jaw wasn't so tight, and his lips softened in a way I couldn't put into words.

I pulled the blanket higher over my shoulder when I felt a draft come into the room.

Crewe opened his eyes when he felt me move, and his gaze was just as intense as always. He watched me without blinking, making sure I wasn't going to leave his side before he relaxed again.

It was like I'd spooked a bear.

We hadn't had dinner yet. When the maid arrived, we ignored the door, and they left us alone. Now I was hungry, but I was far too comfortable to move. I'd rather starve as long as I got to stay in Crewe's arms.

Crewe closed his eyes again, the sound of the fire soothing him to sleep.

I moved my hands up his chest and gently massaged him, feeling the rock-hard muscles that protected me every night I slept by his side. The mood was comfortable until my stomach rumbled loudly.

Crewe didn't open his eyes, but he grinned. "I can take a hint."

"Sorry…"

"It's okay." He rolled me onto my back and fisted my hair in one fluid motion. He gave me a hard kiss before he rose to his feet and grabbed his phone from his pants pocket. He made a call to someone downstairs before he hung up and tossed the phone aside. "It's on the way."

"Good."

He pulled on his sweat pants before he joined me by the fire again. He returned to his spot on the rug and circled his arms around me once more. "Don't eat me, alright?"

I ran my hand up his chest. "I can't promise anything."

The corner of his mouth rose in a smile.

I got comfortable again and studied him, seeing his thick hair coming in around his chin. He had a strong and chiseled jaw, a physicality that reminded me of old-fashioned movie stars. He had a naturally handsome face, clearly born of royalty.

He turned to me when he noticed my stare. "You see something you like?"

"I like all of you." I moved closer into his side and rested my face in the crook of his arm.

He held me close to his chest then pressed a kiss against my temple, a sign of affection he rarely showed. He didn't mention what happened when we made love. I didn't mention it either. I wasn't sure if there was anything to say.

I had him right where I wanted him.

I hadn't thought I'd ever be able to accomplish it.

Making him fall in love with me.

Now I felt innately evil, tricking him into feelings he may not have felt otherwise. I fucked him for months straight, being every fantasy he ever had. I never pushed him on topics that made him uncomfortable, and I was the confidant every man dreamed of. I put aside my own freedom, my sassy comebacks to focus on what was important.

Getting out of there.

But now, it didn't feel like a prison. He didn't feel like a monster. I missed him when he was gone all day. I loved sleeping beside him. I judged myself for softening for a man cruel enough to keep me as his prisoner for six months, but most of it was out of my control. A part of me even wanted to stay.

But I refused to accept that fate.

I just had to figure out my next move. I'd never given it much thought because I didn't think I'd ever get this far. I never thought Crewe would look me in the eye and tell me he loved me.

It was unbelievable.

It rained the next day, so I had nothing to do but stay inside and listen to it pour. Crewe had a private gym, but I preferred to work out outside underneath the blue sky. It made me feel like I had freedom, even if it was wishful thinking.

I cleaned the quarters since I had nothing else to do and took care of Crewe's laundry. I always hoped I would come across the transmitter that was remotely linked to the bomb in Joseph's head, but now that I knew it was all a hoax, I stopped caring about it.

I couldn't believe he'd lied to me for this long.

If he loved me, why hadn't he told me the truth? Why hadn't he offered to let me go? To let me be a private citizen again with my own life? Why was he still keeping me here like this? Was it really love? Or was it just habit?

I wasn't sure.

The fact that he hadn't come clean about anything just hardened my resolve. My heart throbbed when he said those words to me, making me feel higher than a kite, but now I was yanked back down to earth where my shoes hit the hard ground.

His love wasn't enough to give me what I deserved.

The truth.

I walked downstairs in one of the dresses Dimitri had placed in my closet, my hair done and my makeup light. Crewe never said it, but I knew he preferred it when I wore minimal makeup, usually just mascara and a small amount of foundation. He preferred the natural look as opposed to the supermodel look.

I hadn't seen Ariel since their big fight, and I hoped I didn't cross her path anytime soon. The woman wasn't stupid, and she knew I was up to no good. Actually, she hit the nail right on the head. Any interaction with her could just stir up her suspicion.

I approached Crewe's door and came face-to-face with Dimitri. "Can I see him?" I had to check in with his personal bodyguard anytime I wanted anything. I would normally have a thing or two to say about it, but since Crewe's affection was more important than my attitude, I bit my tongue.

Dimitri didn't say a word before he disappeared inside the office. He came back a moment later. "He'll see you now."

"Thanks." I held back the sarcasm before I walked inside.

"Dimitri?" Crewe didn't look up from his desk as he was finishing signing a document.

"Sir?" Dimitri said.

"Lady London can come and go as she pleases." He grabbed another paper and signed the bottom in one quick motion.

Dimitri nodded before he walked out.

I tried not to smile at Crewe's offer, knowing he gave me power no one else in this castle had.

He finished what he was doing and met my gaze, looking handsome in his gray suit and black tie. A glass of water sat on his desk, his scotch nowhere in sight. He even gave me a slight smile, the kind that reached his eyes. "What can I do for you?"

I sauntered to his table, my hips shaking. My fingers touched the top of his desk, and I slid them across the wood as I walked around and parked my ass in his lap. "You're already doing it."

"What am I doing, exactly?"

I brought his fingertips to my lips and kissed them. "Looking fine as hell." I kissed his fingers again before I held them in my lap.

That intense gaze returned to his face, his mocha-colored eyes warm like freshly brewed coffee. "I would take you on this desk, but I have a meeting in ten minutes."

"Then take me after the meeting."

His hands gripped my ass, and he pulled me closer to him. "Consider it a date."

"Ooh…the best date I've ever been on."

When he smiled, he looked like an entirely new man. It was the first time I saw a boyish charm, a playfulness in his eyes that made him cute in a way he never was before. He used to be dark and foreboding, downing scotch left and right and snapping when he was in one of his foul moods.

But now he was happy.

Was that all because of me?

He lifted me onto the desk and kissed me. "Wait right here. I'll be back in an hour."

"An hour?" I asked incredulously. "You're lucky you're worth the wait."

He smiled and kissed me again. "You know I'm good for it." He stepped away, his shoulders broad and powerful. He was about to walk out and leave me there to wait for him.

I came down here for a reason, so I stuck to my plan. "Actually, I wanted to ask for a favor. Since I have time to kill…"

He stopped and placed his hands in his pockets, but he didn't walk back to me. He stood still and tall like a mountain, his strength underneath the surface of that crisp suit. "You know you can ask me for anything, Lovely."

My heart skipped a beat again. My palms were clammy, and my breathing was uneven. He said heartfelt things when I least expected them. The fact that I knew he meant them made it even more meaningful. "I was wondering if I could call my brother…haven't talked to him in a while." I was deliberately playing him for a fool, and now the guilt was growing inside my gut. I shouldn't feel any compassion, but I did. I didn't feel good about what I was doing—at all.

He stared me down for a few more seconds before he pulled his phone out of his pocket and pulled up the number on his screen. He walked to the desk and set it on the surface. "Ten minutes. Dimitri will check on you."

All the guilt disappeared instantly when I heard those words. I had a chaperone to make sure I did what I was told, that I got off the phone with my brother within the ten-minute time frame. The second I asked for a little freedom, he shot it down with an insult.

I forced myself not to speak my mind and stir the pot. He was giving me what I wanted, so there was no point in sabotaging myself. My chance would come. I would get what I deserved all in due time. "Thank you." I had to force myself to spit out the words even though they felt like acid up my throat.

Crewe snaked his hand up my arm until he reached my shoulder. He looked down at me with his handsome face before he pressed a kiss to the corner of my mouth. "I'll be back in an hour. I want you naked on my desk when I come back."

Within the snap of a finger, I was back to being infatuated all over again. Excitement ran through my body in waves, and a tingling sensation formed in my fingertips. I wanted to be naked on that desk right this instant. "Yes, sir."

His eyes narrowed in satisfaction before he walked away. He moved to the door on the other side of the room, ruling me and the entire castle in his silence. With broad shoulders and a powerful physique, he could command anyone that crossed his path. His power was innate and true, stemming from the invisible crown on his head.

When he was finally gone, I grabbed the phone and hit the call button.

It only rang once before Joseph answered. "Yes?" He spoke with his guard up, unsure if it was me or Crewe.

"It's me." I sat in the leather armchair and wondered what it was like for Crewe to sit there every single day. His hard body had pressed against the leather cushions for years, but there still wasn't an outline from his weight. His desk was perfectly organized, and the wood lacked even a speck of dust. It looked too clean ever to have been used.

He didn't sound happy to speak to me. "If you'd just left with me, I wouldn't have had to wait for your call every single day."

"And if I had left with you, you'd be dead right now."

"I'm not so sure," he said coldly. "How are you?"

"Things have been good." I could never go into the details about anything unless I wanted his head to explode.

"Made any progress?"

I eyed the door again even though I was certain I was alone. I brought my voice to a whisper just in case. "One of his men told me the transmitter in your skull is fake."

"Fake?"

"As in, it's not wired to anything."

Joseph paused as he let my words sink in. "What makes you think this guy is being honest?"

"Because he hates me and wants me to leave."

"Hmm…"

"I think he's telling the truth. I don't think Crewe would do something like that."

"Why does this guy hate you?"

"Because I got him demoted since we didn't get along. Now he works outside all night, and I've put a wedge between him and Crewe."

"Good job, sis. Then maybe he is being honest."

"I think so. I don't see what incentive he has to lie."

"Yeah, I don't either. That's good news. I can just ambush him and take you."

"Ambush him?" I asked incredulously.

"Take all of my men and burn that castle to the ground," he said coldly. "They'll never know we're coming."

358 | PENELOPE SKY

Joseph had a violent way of solving problems. Crewe would deserve what was coming to him, but I didn't want that for him. He was a good person despite the evil things he did. All I wanted was to leave peacefully, not get anyone hurt. "We don't need to do that."

"You've got a better idea?"

"Actually, yes. He told me he loved me yesterday."

Joseph paused again. "You're being serious?"

"Yeah."

"Wow. Crewe is a bigger dumbass than I thought."

I felt offended when I shouldn't. "He's not a dumbass. I made it happen."

"He's still an idiot. What are you going to do now?"

There was only one solution, but I didn't know how well Crewe would take it. "I'm gonna talk to him and ask him to let me go."

I could hear Joseph roll his eyes through the phone. "That's not gonna work."

"I think it might."

"No, it won't. You're just gonna spill your secret, and he's gonna keep a tighter leash on you. Shit, he might even kill you. He's got a lot of pride."

Crewe would never kill me. "I'm not gonna spill my secret. I'm just going to ask for more out of the relationship—like freedom. I want the ability to come and go as I please. If he can't give that to me, then he doesn't love me."

"Everyone has a very different definition of love—especially a guy like him."

"I think he means it. He's different with me."

"He's keeping you locked up in a castle. Sounds like a fucking monster to me."

I couldn't argue against that. "Let me do this first."

"And if it goes south? He'll never let you call me again."

No, he wouldn't. "It's not gonna go south."

"But what if it does?" he asked. "I have no way of contacting you."

Based on everything I learned about Crewe, I had to believe he would let me go if I asked. He was compassionate and caring, and we had a deep connection.

I refused to believe he would backhand me and chain me to the floor. "If you don't hear from me in two weeks... come and get me."

"I can get on board with that. Where are you?"

"Sterling Castle outside of Edinburgh."

"Tell me about his crew. Where are their posts? What time do they change shifts?"

I told him everything I knew and what kind of weapons they had. "But if it comes to this, I don't want you to kill anyone. Just make them surrender, get me, and leave. And don't you dare shoot Crewe."

"There's no way I can pull that off. People are gonna get shot."

"Then I don't want to be rescued."

Joseph sighed into the phone. "This guy has really fucked with your mind, London. You shouldn't care if I shoot him between the eyes."

"But I do care." A lot. "I don't want anything to happen to anyone. They're good people just trying to support their families. They're no different from you."

"I would never kidnap anyone for six months," he snapped.

"But you aren't innocent. You crossed him to begin with. Let's not forget how we got into this mess."

All I got from him was silence.

"Those are my terms, Joseph. Give me some time to talk to him."

"What if he moves you?"

"He hasn't mentioned any plans for travel, so I doubt it."

"I doubt he keeps you in the loop about everything," he jabbed.

"Two weeks, okay?"

Joseph didn't say anything.

"Okay?" I pressed. "Two weeks and you choose Plan B."

After another moment of silence, he finally agreed. "Fine. Two weeks."

17

CREWE

London and I hadn't spoken about that night.

The night she told me she loved me.

And I said it back.

I assumed that would open the gates to a long and complicated conversation about our relationship, but that had yet to come. I hoped her confession meant she wanted everything to stay the same, that she enjoyed sharing this enormous castle with me. I wanted our lives to stay exactly the same.

She was the first woman I'd loved since Josephine, and when I compared my feelings for the two women, I questioned whether I loved Josephine at all. I knew I had to marry someone of my stature, and since Josephine was beautiful, I probably just made the best of it.

But with London, it was totally different.

She was everything I wanted in another person. She wasn't royal, but she had class. She wasn't rich, but she was the most intelligent person I'd ever met. She wasn't a suitable partner, but I couldn't picture myself with anyone else.

How did this happen?

She meant nothing to me when she first came into my life. I'd slapped her a few times, kept her in my freezing basement for weeks, and stripped her naked so a stranger could contemplate buying her.

But now she meant everything to me.

I didn't think I was capable of feeling anything like this ever again. I didn't think I could quit being an alcoholic, but she made that happen. I didn't think I could be happy…but she made that happen too.

When I woke up the following morning, I didn't feel like getting any work done. I never took a day off because there was always so much to do, and I felt burned out at the moment. Ariel could cover my calls. And if it was something she couldn't handle, they could wait until tomorrow.

I was usually gone before London opened her eyes, so I took the opportunity to watch her sleep. She abandoned her side of the king bed and hogged mine, her arm wrapped around my waist with her head resting on my chest.

Her back rose and fell as she slept, and her eyelashes looked thick when they were pressed against the top of her cheek. She was naked under the sheets since we went to sleep the second we were finished fucking. My come was still sitting inside her—exactly where it belonged.

Thirty minutes later, her eyes opened and she looked directly into my face. It took her sleepy mind a moment to understand what she was looking at. She blinked then focused her gaze again, my features registering in her brain. "You're still here…"

"I don't feel like working today."

"Are you not feeling well?" she asked, the concern creeping into her voice.

"No, I'm fine. I just want to stay with you."

She stretched her arms and arched her back, her mouth opening with a cute yawn. "A whole day with Crewe?"

"Yeah. How does that sound?"

"That sounds really nice, actually." She pressed kisses along my chest and stomach, her hair trailing across my skin as she moved. "I hope that means I'm gonna get laid."

I smiled, loving how sexy she was without even trying. "You're definitely going to get laid." I rolled on top of her and held my body on top of hers, putting my weight on my elbows. I leaned down and kissed her even though neither one of us had brushed our teeth. It didn't matter what the circumstance was, I always wanted my mouth on hers. She was a fantastic kisser, her small tongue perfect against mine.

She immediately wrapped her legs around my waist, eager to get down to business.

I loved morning sex. Nothing better than having a beautiful woman first thing in the morning. "I love how much you want me."

She hooked her arms around my neck and ground against me. "I've never wanted a man more in my life."

Jesus Christ.

I pushed my cock inside her and slid into that pussy I'd become obsessed with. It was a home for my dick, the space I loved occupying more than any other. Every woman was different, perfect in their own way. But she was far above the rest. I loved every single feature of her body, worshiped it.

Her eyes rolled to the back of her head when she felt me stretch her apart. "Crewe…"

I loved it when my woman said my name. It made me feel more like royalty than my noble blood. My hand snaked into her hair, and I looked into her eyes as I watched her writhe for me. A woman's pleasure wasn't the highest priority on the list, but with London, I wanted to make sure the sex was even better for her than it was for me.

That was probably why she fell in love with me to begin with.

Never in my life had I shared my universe with another person. I had my men and my guards, and I had Finley, who'd been part of my life longer than my own parents. But there was never a real partnership. Even Ariel wasn't someone whom I connected my soul with. When

Josephine and I were engaged to be married, I still didn't feel this way.

With London, she felt like family. She filled the hole my parents' death had left behind. She shared my world and made it a better place. When I walked into our private quarters, I could truly be myself. I didn't have to be the scotch king anymore.

I could just be a man.

The fact that she fell for me despite her difficult situation only told me what we had was real. Only something stronger than lust could bring us together like this. Only something true could get London to look at me the way she was looking at me right now.

Her hands glided up my shoulders until they dug into my hair. Her fingertips were either brutal or gentle, clawing at me or caressing me. She rocked her hips in tune with my thrusts, taking my cock just as I was giving it. She breathed into my mouth as she enjoyed me, her hard nipples rubbing against my chest.

There was nowhere else in the world I'd rather be than here. "So fucking beautiful." I would never get over the fact that she was mine. A lot of beautiful women had graced my bed, but they had nothing on this woman. I could stare at the corner of her mouth forever because even that small part was absolutely perfect. I was obsessed with her body, but I was also obsessed with her soul.

Her eyes melted like chocolate in the summer sun. Her nails dragged down the back of my neck to my shoulders, and she clawed her way into my muscle, her hips still working with mine. Her lips were parted, and her small teeth could be seen. "I love you so much." She pulled me harder into her like she wasn't getting enough of me.

I didn't think twice before the words came out of my mouth. "I love you more." We never had the long and annoying conversation about our future, and I started to suspect it was never coming. London was happy where we are, happy with where we stood in the middle of time. She wanted me every day until our days on earth were gone.

She kissed me and breathed into my mouth at the same time, her excitement palpable. Her ankles locked together around my waist and her nails scratched my skin.

I realized it was the first time I was truly happy. The feeling was so foreign I didn't recognize it. I couldn't remember the last time I was happy. Maybe I'd never been happy all my life. I thought Josephine made me complete, but I quickly realized that was just a short-term high. What I had with London was special. If I met her in a bar on a night out, we probably would have ended up the same way. She didn't need to be my prisoner for us to fall for each other.

It was meant to happen.

We sat together at the table on the balcony, getting a great view of the castle and the hills beyond. It stopped raining yesterday, so the sun was out. It was still chilly, so London wore black leggings and a loose sweater. Even in the bulky clothing, she still looked eye-catching. Her slender neckline and petite shoulders reminded me of everything that existed under the fabric.

We had just finished lunch, and now we enjoyed the comfortable silence between us. She was reading a book, and I was enjoying the view of Scotland and my woman in one look. I wasn't even this comfortable with Ariel, someone I'd known and trusted for a long time. I knew I couldn't marry someone who wouldn't further my political agenda as well as my business goals, but I knew

I would never find this special tranquility again with someone else.

Only with London.

I was happy. I was at peace. They were two sensations I'd never had the honor of enjoying once in my life. Now that I had them, I never wanted to let them go. Marriage wasn't on my mind, but I certainly couldn't let London go.

Not when she changed my life.

Ariel wouldn't be happy, but she'd have to deal with it when the time came.

London cleared her throat then set down her book. Her fingers quickly adjusted her hair even though it wasn't in her face to begin with. She began to squirm, like she was suddenly uncomfortable sitting in the chair. "There's something I want to talk about…"

Maybe I was wrong. Maybe we were going to have a conversation about our future. I was annoyed, but what did I expect? Of course, she wanted to know where we stood. The fact that I told her I loved her should have been pretty clear evidence that I was in this for the long haul. "I'm listening."

She paused as she tried to think of how to begin the conversation. Her eyes shifted back and forth. "Well… I've been here for a while and—"

My phone started to ring on the table. Ariel's name popped up on the screen. I could take advantage of the interruption to ditch the conversation, but that would only postpone it, not get rid of it. I silenced the call. "I apologize. You were saying?"

"I understand if you need to take it, Crewe."

"I'm sure whatever you have to say is more important. She can wait."

Her eyes melted just as they had that morning. She never showed her appreciation that I'd given her as much power as Ariel and Dimitri, but when she looked at me like that, I knew she was touched. "Thanks."

I rested my fingertips against my lips as I waited for her to continue.

"Anyway…I've been here for a long time…seven months. Things are different than they were when I first came here. Obviously, we didn't like each other very much."

I could keep the smile off my face. "No, I wasn't your biggest fan, and you weren't mine."

"Definitely," she said with a chuckle. "I came as your prisoner, and I still am your prisoner…but since things are different—"

Ariel called again. Her name displayed on the screen as the phone vibrated loudly against the tabletop.

I hit the ignore button again. "I'm sorry, Lovely."

"Maybe it's important."

"She can wait until you're finished."

She didn't melt this time, probably put off by being interrupted twice.

"Please continue." I didn't care about interrupting people, but it was obvious London was putting her heart on display, and I didn't want to make her feel foolish. She didn't open up to me very often, and I wanted her to feel comfortable doing it.

She sighed before she continued. "Our relationship is different now, obviously. And I want other things to be different too."

"Such as?" I wasn't sure what she could possibly want. She didn't have a care in the world, and she could have anything she possibly wanted. I would lavish her with expensive clothes, jewelry, and exotic trips around the world.

"For one, I'd like—"

Ariel pounded on the door. I could hear it all the way on the balcony. "Crewe, answer the damn door. We have an emergency on our hands."

Now London had to be cut off. This conversation could wait until another time. "I'm sorry, I have to go." I left the table without saying another word to her, knowing Ariel would never come to my door like this unless it really was an emergency.

London let me go without an argument.

I got to the door in my jeans and t-shirt, something Ariel hardly ever saw me in. "What is it?"

She didn't waste time with a smartass comment about me blowing off work today. "Pias sent our shipment to Istanbul, but it was intercepted."

"Intercepted?" I blurted.

"Yes. By pirates. Everything was lost."

That was a huge blow to our deal. Millions of dollars of product were on that ship. "Jesus Christ."

"Come on, let's go."

I shut the door behind me and followed her.

18

LONDON

I picked the wrong time to have my conversation with Crewe. If I had just done it a few hours before, I would have had his undivided attention. But he was gone with Ariel all day and most of the night. He didn't call to check in, so I had no idea when he would be back.

Bad timing.

The stress of the situation was getting to me because I really had no idea how he would react. In my heart, I believed he cared enough about me that he wouldn't hurt me after I made my request. He would be understanding and compassionate. He would understand he couldn't keep me as a prisoner forever.

We couldn't stay like this.

I had my own dreams and ambitions. I couldn't be his plaything forever.

If he loved me, he would let me go.

And I believed he did love me—in his own way.

Crewe returned at three in the morning. I knew he was home because I hadn't been able to sleep without him beside me. I tossed and turned constantly, the sheets feeling cold without the heat of his body to keep me warm throughout the night. I was used to having sex before bed, so that threw me off too.

He walked inside and tried to shut the door as quietly as he could, assuming I was asleep.

I sat up in bed wearing one of his t-shirts and sweat pants. I usually slept in just my underwear, but that was too cold when I was sleeping alone. "Everything okay?"

He stilled at the sound of my voice then flicked on the light near the doorway so he wouldn't have to walk around in the dark. "Yeah. We retrieved the shipment."

"How did you manage that?"

He ran his hand through his hair and kicked off his shoes at the same time. After working for over twelve hours, he probably didn't want to talk about it, but he didn't show me any attitude. "I've got eyes and ears all over the world."

I didn't leave the bed because I knew he would join me once his clothes were off. "Sorry that happened."

"Not your fault. No one's fault, really." He pulled his phone out of his pocket and set it on the nightstand. "I know you were trying to tell me something earlier, but can it wait until the morning? I'm out of it right now."

"Of course—"

A gunshot rang through the air.

Crewe stilled, his eyes immediately moving to the window.

A machine gun sounded in the distance, echoing across the castle walls. It was coming from outside, near the entrance.

Joseph.

There wasn't a doubt in my mind he was here. He said he would give me two weeks, but he had obviously changed his mind. He probably assumed I was crazy for wanting to protect Crewe. His anger had blinded his judgment, and now he was the one who was crazy.

Crewe immediately sprang into action. He opened one of his drawers and pulled out a pistol. He checked the barrel to make sure it was loaded before he shoved it into the back pocket of his jeans. "Come on."

"What are we doing?" I jumped out of bed, my heart racing a million miles a minute. I was more scared than the day I was originally captured. Joseph was here to take me, and he didn't give a damn about sparing Crewe's life.

Shit.

He grabbed my hand and pulled me to his side. He didn't bother putting his shoes back on. "I'm gonna get us out of here."

"Maybe it's safer if we stay in here?"

"Doubt it. Whoever is here is looking for me." He opened the door and stepped into the hallway, the sound of gunshots even louder. It sounded like a gang war was waging outside. "And they won't hesitate to kill you too."

I knew I was safe, but that didn't stop me from being terrified. Now that Crewe's life was on the line, I could hardly breathe. I gripped his hand tighter, unable to handle the possibility of something happening to him. I didn't care about any of his men, but I didn't want anything to happen to them either—not even Ariel. "Where are we going?"

"There's an escape route on the other side of the castle."

"What about everyone else?"

He pulled me into another hallway and approached a second staircase. "They know what they're supposed to do."

"Ariel?"

"She knows where the secret room is. She'll be fine."

I hoped so.

He pulled me down the staircase just as the large glass window that led to the courtyard was shattered by bullets. It burst into shards and blanketed the maroon rug that led down the stone hallway.

Crewe yanked me to the floor and protected my body with his.

This couldn't be happening. This was a nightmare. The worst nightmare I'd ever had.

Crewe was on his feet an instant later, firing his weapon at any enemies I couldn't see. He took one down and another fired, but he dodged out of the way behind the staircase, taking me with him.

"It's him." Joseph's voice rang in the air. "He's got her with him."

Crewe's held his gun at the ready and didn't react, but he must have figured out who it was.

"Let her go, asshole." Joseph cocked his gun. I could hear the sound echo against the stone.

Crewe was outnumbered three to one. It didn't matter how smart or fast he was. He couldn't get out of this. Gunshots still fired from outside the walls, Crewe's men engaged in the battle to keep the rest of Joseph's men out. It was merely a distraction so Joseph could enter through the back.

Crewe kept his hand firmly on mine, looking eerily calm for the dire situation he was in.

"I'm coming out," I announced. "Don't shoot."

Crewe gripped me tighter and looked down at me.

I avoided his look and slipped out of his grasp, knowing there was no time to explain anything. Now his life was on the line, and I had to do whatever I could to spare it. I stepped out with my arms by my sides, relieved when I wasn't shot even though I was never a target. "Joseph, tell your men to stand down."

Joseph looked maniacal, his eyes wide. His eyes were just as dark as the bulletproof vest he wore. "Come here."

I held my ground. "Drop your weapons."

"We aren't gonna shoot you," he hissed. "Now get your ass over here."

"Don't shoot Crewe. I told you I didn't want anyone to get hurt. Tell your men to stop. You won. Now let's go." Crewe didn't need to hear the backstory to understand what my words meant. I'd plotted this entire thing with Joseph during those phone calls, and now he knew what I was really up to.

Joseph lowered his weapon, as did the others. "Let's go, then."

I breathed a sigh of relief now that I had accomplished the most important thing—protecting Crewe.

"Are you gonna show your face, you coward?" Joseph asked. "Say goodbye to the slave you've kept for seven months?" Spit flew from his mouth, and the vein in his forehead throbbed. His anger was hotter than a raging wildfire. I could feel the ferocity from my fingertips to my toes.

Crewe stepped out from behind the staircase, his gun hanging by his side. But he didn't look at Joseph once. All he did was look at me.

With fury.

With pain.

With betrayal.

His jaw was tighter than I'd ever seen it, and the devastation in his eyes made me feel worse than he had ever made me feel. There wasn't a fight inside him. He didn't even care that Joseph was standing there with two armed men. He showed more vulnerability in that moment than I'd ever seen him show during our relationship. "You got me."

"You actually thought she loved you?" Joseph asked incredulously. "You took this woman as a prisoner. How stupid are you? If you didn't think my sister would fight every single day to get out, you really are an idiot."

Crewe didn't take his eyes off me. "You're right. I am an idiot."

"It wasn't like that," I whispered. "I was going to talk to you—"

Joseph raised his gun and fired, shooting Crewe right in the chest. "Die, asshole."

"No!" My hands moved to my face when I saw Crewe jerk before he crashed to the floor. His body hit the stone with a loud thump, and he lay still, his eyes still open and blood spraying into the air in front of him. His t-shirt started to become soaked, and his arms lay by his sides.

Joseph stood over him and pointed the gun right at Crewe's face.

"Stop!" I covered Crewe's body with my own, protecting as much of him as I could. "Joseph, stop! You told me you wouldn't kill him."

Joseph lowered the gun and shrugged. "Well, I changed my mind. Now, move."

"No." Tears immediately poured from my eyes, and I sobbed as I felt Crewe's blood absorb into my own clothes. "Get away from him." I kicked Joseph in the shin so he would stumble backward.

One of his men got a message through the speaker in his ear. "Crewe's reinforcements are on the way. There's a lot of them. We're outnumbered ten to one. We've got to go."

Thank god.

Joseph rubbed his chin but didn't give any indication he was in pain. "London, we've got to go."

"I'm not leaving. I'm getting him to a hospital."

"Are you crazy?" He grabbed me by the arm.

I smacked him away then bit him on the forearm when he grabbed me again. "Leave!"

"I risk my life for you, and this is how you repay me?" my brother asked.

"I told you not to shoot him, Joey! You did it anyway. Now, go." I grabbed Crewe's gun and pointed it right at my brother. "Don't call my bluff, Joseph." My hand didn't shake, and I wouldn't hesitate to shoot him right in the chest if he made me.

Joseph knew me well enough to understand I was serious. "Let's go." He led the way as they headed to the entrance, his men following behind him.

I dropped the gun and immediately focused on Crewe, my training kicking in on instinct. I ripped his shirt with my bare hand and saw the wound in his chest. Blood was pouring out, and it was dangerously close to his heart.

I got the shirt off then examined the wound. The bullet didn't pierce his heart, but it was close enough that I was concerned it had pierced his chest cavity. If I didn't get him to a hospital immediately, he would bleed out and die. Without a CT scan, there was no way for me to know the extent of the damages. I left the bullet in place because removing it could hurt his chances of survival. I tied the shirt over his shoulder and across his chest, trying to stay calm even though I couldn't stop sobbing.

Crewe stared at me with indifference, as if he didn't feel anything. He didn't show pain or anger. Only indifference. "Just leave, London." He stared at the ceiling, refusing to look at me. "You have what you want. Just go."

"No." I secured the shirt and stopped the bleeding as much as I could. My palms were slick because they were soaked in his blood.

"Just. Go." With strength that came from nowhere, he shoved me off him. "I mean it."

"No." I grabbed the rug underneath him and began to pull. "You're gonna be okay. Just stay calm." He was so heavy I could barely pull him. My fingers kept slipping on the material, and my back ached because I wasn't equipped for this.

"I am calm," he said with indifference. "Leave me here to die—exactly like you wanted."

"You know that's not what I wanted." I dug my feet into the stone and pulled him harder, slowly getting momentum. I had to drag him hundreds of feet to the other side of the castle. "I need you to stop talking, Crewe. I need to you to stay calm."

"Trust me, I'm calm."

My fingers slipped, and I fell to the ground, my entire body aching from pulling him. I turned around and searched for help, hoping one of his men could loan me their strength. "Hello? Somebody help."

"Just go," Crewe repeated.

I came back to him, the panic rising even more. "I need you to walk for me, okay? I know you can do it."

He stared at the ceiling, refusing to look at me. "Yeah, I can walk. But I'm not going to."

The tears poured harder down my face. "Crewe…"

"Just. Leave. Me."

"Crewe—"

"Enough." He silenced me with just a word, his eyes glued to the ceiling.

I ran to the front door and burst outside, seeing Joseph's men quickly piling into their trucks. I spotted Ariel on the ground with her arms handcuffed behind her back. One man grabbed her by the neck and yanked her to her feet.

No.

I pulled out Crewe's gun and aimed it at the man. "Let her go."

Ariel looked at me with a new glare of hatred. It was more powerful than any other glares she ever gave me.

I pushed the gun into his face. "I said let her go. Now."

He turned to Joseph, who hopped out of the truck.

Joseph stared me down with annoyance. "An eye for an eye."

"You shot him!" I yelled. "The score is even. You aren't taking her. Now, let her go. I don't have time for this."

Joseph shook his head. "You're lucky I didn't shoot that asshole in the head. Be grateful."

I aimed the gun at this his chest. "Let her go. I'm not fucking around, Joseph."

Joseph finally nodded to the man to release her. "I'm leaving. This is your last chance to get out of here."

I watched the guard uncuff her. "I'm staying right here."

Ariel was finally released from her handcuffs, and the first thing she did was punch me in the face. "You fucking whore."

I didn't feel anything because I was numb to the pain. And I deserved it.

Joseph didn't retaliate.

"Crewe has been shot. He's too heavy for me to carry. I need your help getting him to the hospital."

The second Ariel heard that information, she lowered her hand and stopped attacking me. Her mentality changed, turning from anger to pragmatism. "Where is he?"

"Follow me." I ran inside and led her to where he lay on the rug in the grand hallway. "Help me pull him."

Ariel gripped one edge and began to pull. "Crewe, I'm here."

Crewe stared at the ceiling.

Ariel pulled the rug with me, but we weren't making as much progress as I had when it was just me. She gave up and kneeled beside him. "Crewe, I need you to walk. Now."

"No." Crewe didn't look at her either. "You were right about her. I'm sorry."

Ariel grabbed his hand. "I know how you feel right now. But we need to get you to the hospital. You're gonna bleed out and die."

I stood back because I knew I wouldn't be any help. I would just make it worse.

"Then let me die," he said simply.

Ariel stared at him hard then leaned down and whispered in his ear. I had no idea what she said. Perhaps she spoke of something only the two of them knew about.

I hoped it was enough to get him up.

Crewe lay there for a few more seconds before he finally sat up, his movements wobbly because he had already lost so much blood.

I cried harder when I saw him get up. "Thank god…"

Ariel hooked her arm around him and helped him to the door. "Get a car."

I sprinted outside and found a Jeep parked along the grass. The engine was still running, but it had been abandoned by Crewe's men. I got the back door open and watched Ariel get him inside. She took the seat beside him and placed her hand over his chest, keeping the pressure on. "Drive, bitch."

I hauled ass away from the castle and drove straight into the city. I knew we weren't far from the rest of civilization, but I had no idea where the hospital was.

Ariel directed me. "Make a left here."

I turned and sped through traffic, cutting off anyone who got in my way. I accidentally scraped against a parked car on the side of the road, but that didn't stop me.

"Right," Ariel commanded.

I nearly hit a person in the crosswalk, but luckily they dodged out of the way. I finally pulled into the entrance of the hospital, the roundabout where the emergency department was. "We're here."

"I can see that," Ariel hissed. She threw the door open and helped Crewe out.

But he stumbled until his knees hit the ground.

"Crewe!" I rushed to him, leaning over him, seeing his eyes close. "Stay awake. Come on, stay awake." I slapped his cheeks to make his eyes open again.

Ariel sprinted inside and got the attention of the staff. They ran out with a stretcher and a team of doctors and nurses, getting him on the gurney and rushing into the department.

I jogged after the gurney, seeing them push him through the double doors and out of my sight.

Ariel stopped when security told her to turn back.

She stood in front of the double doors with her hands on her hips, her arms covered with blood. She slowly turned around and looked at me, her eyes acting as two guns. If she could shoot me and get away with it, she would.

And I knew I deserved it.

***

Ariel and I stayed away from each other.

One by one, Crewe's men arrived at the hospital. Dunbar was one of them, and fortunately, he hadn't been injured. But from his report to Ariel, they'd lost a few men in the attack.

I felt worse.

Dunbar stared at me coldly from Ariel's side, his glare just as terrifying as hers.

The longer I stayed, the more I put myself in danger. Crewe's team wouldn't hesitate to kill me after what I did. I betrayed him and everyone else. They didn't understand that I never wanted Joseph to storm the castle like that. They didn't understand that I specifically told Joseph not to hurt anyone, especially Crewe.

Hours passed, and we didn't hear anything. The nurse said he'd been rushed to emergency surgery, complications from the bullet lodged in his chest. He probably had internal bleeding along with a few broken ribs.

I hoped he would be okay.

I hoped he would make it through.

I cried on and off as I waited in the emergency room, my arms tight across my chest. If he didn't make it, I wouldn't know what to do with myself. I did what was necessary to be free again, but now that he wasn't with me, I didn't feel free at all.

I was trapped all over again.

Hours turned into days. I didn't sleep because I couldn't leave, not when I didn't know if he was going to be okay. More of Crewe's men arrived at the hospital, but that didn't scare me off. They lost some of their comrades because of me, so of course, they wanted me dead. Even when the threat grew bigger and bigger, I still didn't leave. I didn't sleep either.

Finally, a doctor came out and walked up to Ariel.

I rushed to her side, not caring if she slapped me or pushed me away. I needed an update on Crewe, to know he was still breathing.

Ariel gave me a fiery look but didn't tell me to leave.

"We got the bullet out and patched up the severed artery," the doctor explained. "We gave him a transfusion because he lost a lot of blood. There weren't any other complications, so he's going to pull through. We're going to keep him for a few more days to monitor his progress, but I think he'll be okay. As long as there's no infection, he should be alright."

I covered my face as I felt a new wave of hot tears emerge. They dripped down my face and coated my lips. I knew everyone was staring at me, but I didn't care. Relief washed over me in waves. "Thank god..."

"Thank you, Dr. Mitchel," Ariel said as she dismissed him.

He walked away, leaving us alone together.

I pulled my hands down and looked at her, unashamed of how ugly I looked at that moment. Now that Crewe was okay, she was probably going to threaten me. The second I left that hospital, I was dead meat.

"You have no right to be here." She had a tiny drop of blood on her cheek, probably Crewe's that she hadn't noticed yet. "You got what you wanted, so now you need to leave."

I wanted to see him, but I didn't know what I would say. Everything was different now. He knew I played him, and even if I told him I cared about him, it wouldn't make a difference. The relationship I enjoyed was gone. He didn't trust me anymore—not that he should. There was nothing keeping me there. While I wished things had worked out differently, my desire was the same. I wanted to be a free woman, and now I was. "I didn't mean for it to happen this way. I told Joseph to back off. I wanted to talk to Crewe myself—"

"I really don't give a shit," she said coldly. "I knew what you were doing long ago. I warned Crewe, but he didn't listen to me. Now some of our men are dead, and Crewe nearly died too. You outsmarted the most intelligent man I know, so congratulations. But you no longer have a purpose here. Enjoy your freedom."

My feet remained glued to the tile. I could hear the quiet conversations around me, people concerned about their loved ones while sitting in the emergency room. I heard some of Crewe's men speak on the phone, instructing other men what to do while their leader was incapacitated. "I know you're going to kill me, so I don't have any freedom."

Her eyes narrowed like I'd said something new to offend her. "You wanna know what I whispered to Crewe?"

Actually, I did. I nodded, surprised she would share that information with me.

"I told him I was going to kill you if he didn't get to his feet. I threatened to cause you as much pain as possible if he didn't do everything he possibly could to get to the hospital. That's why he got up, London. That's why he's alive right now—to protect you."

19

LONDON

Joseph picked me up at the hospital. There was a silent declaration of a truce between Crewe's men and him since he was only removing me from the situation with no intention of causing any further damage.

I wouldn't have called him—but I had no one else.

He drove me to a hotel near the airport so I could get some sleep. I hadn't closed my eyes in forty-eight hours, and now that I knew Crewe was okay, I could finally rest my head against a pillow.

Joseph left because he had to take care of my paperwork to make sure I could catch a flight when I woke up. So

400 | PENELOPE SKY

far, we had said very little to each other. He was pissed at me, and I was just as pissed at him.

But we were still family.

When I woke up the next day, Joseph gave me all my paperwork, along with something else. "I've set up an account in your name in the US. It has more than enough to cover any expenses that you have." He handed me the card as well as the account information.

"Joseph, you don't need to give me any money."

"It's gonna take you some time to put your life back together. Trust me, you'll need it."

Knowing Joseph, it was probably a fortune. "I'll pay you back."

"You don't need to pay me back," he said quickly. "Do you want me to fly out with you? I can help you get settled back in New York."

There was nothing I wanted more. I would love to have him for support as I moved back home and put my life back together. But I knew he had more important things to do here. "I'll be fine."

"You're sure?" he pressed.

"Yeah."

"What are you going to do?"

I hadn't thought about how I was going to spend my freedom. All I'd been thinking about was Crewe's well-being. "I don't know...probably go back to school. If I have to wait until next year, I'll probably take the physician assistant test and get my license."

He nodded like he understood, even if he didn't. "Not a bad idea."

"No."

He slid his hands into his pockets as he stared at me. "Well, I got you a flight that leaves in a few hours. I should probably drop you off."

"Yeah...it might take me a while to get through customs." I was eager to get to New York, but I was scared to leave this place. I was scared to leave Crewe behind for good. Now that I was truly free, he was all I could think about. I wondered if he'd woken up yet. I wondered if he was thinking about me. I wondered if he would ever forgive me for what I did to him.

Joseph continued to watch me. "You know...you can always talk to me. I know things got out of hand the other night, but I was just angry. I was angry for what he did to you. But I can be calm now that I know you're okay."

I knew Joseph didn't want to listen to me talk about Crewe. He would always hate that man for what he put me through. The fact that he offered was sweet. It sounded exactly like something my brother would do. "I'll keep that in mind."

"Okay. Are you ready to go, then?"

I held my ticket in my hand, feeling my pulse quicken. "Yeah…I think so."

———

Fall had hit New York, and the leaves were changing from vibrant green to red and gold. The air turned crisp and cold, and the tourists left the great city to return to their lives all over the world. I'd been gone for so long that I thought I wouldn't remember where everything was, but it felt like home the second I was back.

Joseph put an incredible sum into my bank account, so I was able to get a nice apartment right off the bat. I furnished it without breaking the bank and having to stress about putting food on the table.

I checked in with my university, and they said I had to wait until the following fall to resume my coursework. So I was losing an entire year of my education even though I'd never wanted to leave my education in the first place.

I knew I should work on getting a job, but I didn't have the motivation for it at the moment.

I kept thinking about him.

Crewe.

I reconnected with my friends, and everyone was relieved to have me back at home. No one asked too many prying questions about what I went through, knowing it was something no one would be able to talk about without choking up.

But I didn't feel like I went through the trauma they assumed I did.

Yes, I'd been captured.

Kept as a prisoner against my will.

But when I thought of Crewe, I didn't think of a monster.

I thought of a friend.

A confidant.

A lover.

A lover whom I missed.

I knew those misplaced feelings would go away in time. Once I was acclimated to New York again, those old feelings would disappear altogether. I wouldn't think about those kisses, the two instances he told me he loved me, and the stone halls I would never pass through again.

I would forget about him eventually.

At least, I hoped I would.

ALSO BY PENELOPE SKY

Their story continues in Worship Your Queen

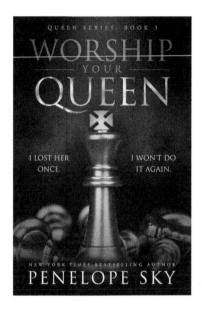

Order Now

Printed in Great Britain
by Amazon

38552268R00233